Haz

Tabitha A Lane

This is a work of fiction. Names, characters, places and incidents are the product of the author's imagination or are used fictiously, and any resemblance to actual persons living or dead, business establishments, events, or locales, is entirely coincidental.

Hazzard Blue

Cover: LM Creations

COPYRIGHT © Tabitha A Lane 2015.

All rights reserved. No part of this book may be used or reproduced in any manner whatsoever without written permission of the author, except in the case of brief quotations embedded in critical articles or reviews.

This book is sold subject to the conditions that it shall not, by way of trade or otherwise, be lent, hired out, or otherwise circulated without the author's prior consent in any form of binding or cover other than that in which it is published and without a similar condition including this condition being imposed on the subsequent purchaser.

ISBN-13: 978-1505687613
ISBN-10: 1505687616

Dedication

For K.Rufon. My inspiration!

Chapter One

A cacophony of sound blared through the apartment. Ring, pause, and repeat, in an endless loop. Someone was leaning on the doorbell, then taking a brief break and stabbing it repeatedly, like a woodpecker having an epileptic fit.

Daniel Hunt crawled out of bed. His employer paid the rent on the New York crash pad he used for stopovers, and no-one ever visited. The ringing was accompanied by a couple of good thumps on the door—it sounded like a crazy person was trying to get in.

He flexed his fingers and formed a fist, then ripped the door open with his other hand. "What?" He was yelling. Damn sure his hair was standing up all over like a wild man. Dressed in a pair of black silk boxers and nothing else.

Cain took a step back.

"Jesus." His eyes were wide. "Cool it, man."

Daniel blinked. "What the hell are you doing here?" His brother was based in San Jose; he'd never visited the New York crash pad. "How did you even know I'm in the country?" Daniel turned away from his brother and stalked into the kitchen in search of coffee.

Cain scampered along behind, like an over-exited

puppy. "Sergei's assistant. She told me you'd be here, and gave me directions." He spoke fast, the words chasing each other out. "I've got news, I've got awesome news. You won't believe it but…"

Daniel swirled around and stuck his hand over Cain's mouth. "I'm tired." He spoke slowly, deliberately. "I've had four hours sleep, and I can't take you being all *enthusiastic*." He ladled as much sarcasm as he could into the last word. "Whatever it is, let me get caffeinated first." He took his hand away.

Cain's mouth opened.

"Na—" Daniel threatened him with the hand again, and Cain's mouth snapped closed.

Cain pointed across the room. "Turn on the TV." His eyes pleaded.

"Fine." Daniel picked up the remote and turned the TV on. "What channel?"

"Any channel." Cain was wigging as if he needed to pee. Moving from foot to foot the way he used to do when he was an excited kid.

Daniel punched in the news channel. Cain pointed at the breaking news ticker along the bottom of the screen.

SOCIAL MEDIA GIANT PAYS FIFTY MILLION DOLLARS FOR SIXTY PERCENT SHARE OF 'BIGTALK'

"Forgive me for waking you up now?"

There was nothing to eat in the apartment so they went out for breakfast. Cain had always been green—shit, even at twenty-six, he was just a kid. A geeky kid at that. Daniel didn't understand the fixation with social media, but as his wide-eyed brother explained that the new social network he and his friend Ben had developed was growing at a rate of half a million new subscribers a day, he realized he should have paid more attention, because people were paying attention to his little brother now. A lot of people. Cain and Ben were like chum thrown into the ocean behind a fishing boat and the sharks were circling.

"My phone has been ringing off the hook since the deal broke," Cain said. "You wouldn't believe the people who have called me."

Daniel arched an eyebrow.

"Women." Cain's face was pink and his eyes were over bright. "Women never call me."

"What women?"

"Every girl I chased in high school. And college. Remember Jenny Merino? She called this morning."

Daniel had spent more than one night in Jenny Merino's bed back when he was a teenager. She was five years older than his little brother and had been one of the hottest girls in school. She'd never shown the slightest interest in Cain, but money changed everything, especially when stacked up in multi-million piles.

He examined at Cain with narrowed eyes. "Isn't she married?"

"She told me she's been separated for six months. She rang to congratulate me and to ask if I'd like to meet up for a drink."

Neither of the Hunt brothers had any guidance in their lives. Money, but no guidance. Daniel's hands clenched into fists as the memory of their father intruded. He'd failed Cain once; it was inconceivable that he'd let anyone use his brother now. He resisted the urge to comment, and returned to the matter at hand. "You need an expert guiding you with the money, helping you to manage it."

"I know." Cain ordered another coffee. "We have a few candidates lined up, but you know what you always say about me—that people take advantage?" He chewed on a piece of bacon. "Well, I know that's true. And Ben's no better. We focus on the software, on the company. I don't want to have to deal with all the other stuff. We need a real tough, take-no-shit guy who we *know* is on our side. But one who can navigate in the business world without coming over as an asshole."

"Any idea who?" Daniel was unsettled at the thought of Cain being controlled by some shark in a suit. The temptation of being in charge of much money was bound to corrupt even the most honorable candidate.

Daniel rubbed a hand over the soft, longer-than-stubble-and-just-about-a-beard on his jaw. He would only trust one guy with the job—himself. His two-year contract piloting Sergei Romanoff's private plane around the world was almost at an end. Sergei had been pushing Daniel to extend the contract—but he was loath to do so. He'd already worked for Sergei longer than he'd ever worked for anyone before. He hated being tied down.

"How about me?"

The relieved light in Cain's eyes confirmed Daniel's suspicions.

"Do you think you might do it?" Cain smiled like a Labrador lying in the sunshine. "That's why I'm here. Ben and I agreed you'd be the perfect person, the perfect buffer between us and everyone else."

"I'm not a money man, you'd have to hire a manager too," Daniel warned.

"We would." Cain nodded. "And you could oversee things. You're the only person I know who won't be influenced by any of this craziness—you'll give us good advice and keep us from being ripped off. We'll pay you an awesome salary."

"My contract with Sergei still has a couple of weeks to run."

"But after that…" Desperate hope was written in Cain's eyes. Hope that Daniel couldn't possibly deny. He couldn't abandon his brother to someone who was motivated purely by money—had to rise to the challenge. He was the only person who would have Cain's welfare as their primary concern.

"I'll talk to him today, see if I can get out of the contract early," Daniel said. "So what are you going to do to celebrate?"

Cain grinned. "We sat up all night talking about that. Top of the list is a total reenactment of our favorite movie."

*****

There was a fucking *rip* in the Aubesson.

Kathryn Hazzard got down on her hands and knees and brought her nose to within an inch of the antique carpet. She traced the broken threads with the tip of her index finger. The carpet was impossible to keep in perfect condition, and it was natural that a carpet that had stayed in the same position for two hundred and fifty years would suffer some wear and tear, but the rip was in a position that got a fair bit of traffic. It would need repair.

She puffed out a frustrated breath. And that meant she'd have to pay a specialist conservator to do the work on-site. A very expensive conservator. Yet another job to add to the horribly-expensive-but-necessary-repairs list. A list that grew by the day. A list she had no hope of getting on top of. Not for the first time, she wished that this old house wasn't her responsibility. That she could just break the bonds of time and family that tethered her, sell the thing and be done with it.

"Why are you waving your ass in the air?" A familiar voice from the doorway.

Kathryn glanced over her shoulder, and smiled. "Rip in the carpet." She sat back on her heels, as her best friend, Maxine Goode walked over. "Help me up, will you?"

Maxine gazed at the rip as she extended a hand. "It's not a very bad one."

"Bad enough. I'll have to get it fixed." Kathryn brushed her knees as she stood. "I'm glad to see you." She hugged her friend close. "I can't take any more shit today."

"What's happened?"

"The painting didn't sell." Nerves roiled in Kathryn's gut. "And as it's appeared in an auction, it's burned for at least six months. The architect's report came in on the roof, and it's worse than I ever imagined—he says if work isn't done in the next couple of months we could be looking at a collapse." She eyed at the white box Max carried. "So I hope to hell you brought chocolate cake."

"Yup." Max held the box high. "I've done more than that. I've brought a solution to all your problems. Make me coffee and I'll tell you."

Hazzard Hall had been in Kathryn's family for two hundred and fifty years, and she was just the latest of a long line of Hazzards tethered to the old wreck in the middle of the English countryside. People always thought the Hazzards owned Hazzard Hall when in fact the complete opposite was true. It owned them. The first Hazzards built it, and subsequent generations had added to it, until the money ran out and the situation reversed.

Her mother had died, abandoning her husband, her only child and the house years ago. Her father had sold off paintings, bronzes, and furniture in an attempt to stem the tide, but his efforts were hopeless. He'd died a broken man—but at least he died in his beloved house.

He'd been dead three months. Kathryn had a team of expensive lawyers calculating the bill she'd have to pay to the tax collectors and no money to pay it.

The house was a nightmare, but it had always been home. On returning from school, and later college, the house welcomed her within its walls. Hazzard was her home. Her castle. Her safe haven. She didn't want to be the Hazzard who gave it all up. The one that sold out. And the fact that its roof was shot to hell meant she wouldn't get anything near its true value if she put it on the market.

In the kitchen, Max sliced wedges off the thick chocolate cake she'd brought. "You need to chill out. You look like shit."

"I feel like shit." Kathryn sank onto the nearest chair in the kitchen. "I'm seriously considering getting drunk and staying that way for the foreseeable future."

"Come on." Max frowned. "That's not like you."

She'd always been a glass half full girl, but there was little point in being optimistic any longer. She was totally screwed. "The taxman cometh." She tried to inject some humor into her tone, but failed miserably. "The roof is about to fall in, and my only hope for getting my hands on some cash is gone. If I don't end up in prison for non-payment of taxes, can I come live with you?"

"What if I told you I have a solution to all your

problems?" Max fixed her with a stare.

"I'd tell you to stop kidding around. And I'd add that you're a bitch to wind me up when I'm at my lowest point."

"I'm not kidding." Max breathed out. She clutched her hands together. "I have a client who wants to use the house for one night. A client willing to pay a million to do so."

She couldn't breathe. Couldn't make sense of the words her friend had spoken. Kathryn pressed the palm of her hand against her breastbone. "A million?"

Max nodded. "One million."

"Pounds?"

"Dollars. The client saw Sex Lies and wants to re-enact it. For real. In Hazzard Hall."

"Sex Lies?" She'd allowed the house to be used as a location for movies in the past, and a year ago, while her father was having treatment in a clinic in Switzerland, she'd let the house be the location for a film about a sex club in a country house. The director was a Hollywood great—a pretty twisted Hollywood great—but she'd needed the money for her father's treatment.

"No-one was supposed to know where the film was shot." She'd insisted on that. They'd never shown the house's exterior, and made no mention of the location in the movie's credits.

"They came direct to the location scout." Max pointed at herself.

"So, let me get this straight." The tips of Kathryn's fingers tingled. A million dollars would get the taxman off her back and give her some money to repair the roof. "They want to use Hazzard Hall to make another film? And will pay a million dollars for a day's shooting?"

Max shook her head. "They're stinking rich, and they want to hold a sex party in your house. One night. One million bucks."

"Fuck me."

*****

Kathryn smoothed a hand over her black silk dress and inhaled deeply. She'd travelled up to London by train, but had splurged and taken a taxi to the exclusive London hotel, rather than the Underground. The spring day was warm, but the clouds bruised grey with threatened rain. Once she'd picked her jaw up from the floor at Max's proposition, she'd been torn, buffeted with conflicting emotions. She'd justified the previous use of Hazzard by telling herself it was make believe. Just a film. But this would be different.

She needed money. A million dollars would make her problems disappear in an instant. But at what personal cost? Hazzard Hall was more than just a house. When she sat in the drawing room in front of the fire, layered decades of precious memories colored the air, enriching every single moment.

Generations of Hazzards had taken tea by the fire. Could she replace those with memories of half-naked strangers screwing on the camelback sofas?

Max had been sympathetic—up to a point. She'd urged Kathryn not to say no, not to reject the possibility of salvation because she couldn't get past the slightly seedy nature of the transaction. "Your dad would have told you to consider every option to save Hazzard," Max had said.

But Kathryn could bet he'd never been asked to prostitute his home.

So she hadn't said yes, and she hadn't said no. She hadn't, in fact, said anything that she would allow Max to repeat to the client. She'd been waiting for the answer to drop out of the sky. She'd looked for it in all the usual places, her horoscope, analyzing her dreams with a what-does-it-mean-if-you-dream-of…website.

After a week, the client's patience had run out. Max had called with an ultimatum. "The clients' representative, Daniel Hunt, is flying in to London from New York on Friday. He wants to meet you."

She really didn't know what she was going to say to the mysterious Mr. Hunt, but had to make this meeting.

Kathryn pushed open the door to the luxury hotel and strode to the reception desk. While she waited for the receptionist to check in the couple ahead of her, she cast an eye around the opulent surroundings. There were a few people in the lobby, one, a tall, silver-haired gentleman who looked as though he was waiting for someone. *God, could that be him?*

She frowned. She hadn't even considered that the group might be in their seventies. She couldn't hold back a shudder as the man turned and smiled, or the relief that flooded her as she realized his attention was on the woman behind her.

Not him, then.

There were two other people in the lobby. One was a nervous blonde woman and the other a tall, dark man, dressed in a finely tailored slate-grey suit. He watched her intently.

He didn't look like a typical London businessman; his hair was too long for that. She'd never really gone for guys with beards, but the dark dusting on his jawline was damned attractive. His skin was tanned and his eyes were glittering green emerald. He was classically handsome, with an edge. A dangerous edge. Maybe it was the prominent cheekbones, maybe the sensuous curve of his mouth, maybe the wide shoulders and narrow hips and the way he stood. Like a big cat, feigning a relaxed state, when in reality he was on the prowl, ready to pounce.

A good girl would turn away. Would act as though she hadn't noticed the sexual interest evident in his eyes. She certainly wouldn't encourage him.

She'd never been a good girl.

Kathryn's nipples tightened against the black lace of her bra. She was safe. Here for a business meeting. It had been months since she'd last had a lover, but there was nothing wrong with window-shopping, was there?

She didn't look away. She smiled slowly and intimately, let her eyes transmit the powerful message that she liked what she saw. When the meeting was over, if he was still here, maybe she'd let him buy her a drink.

The man's eyes widened almost imperceptibly, then an answering smile transformed his features from dangerous to deadly.

Her pulse was racing as she looked away and stepped up to the desk. "I'm here to see Mr. Hunt," she said to the receptionist. "Could you call his room please?"

Chapter Two

Daniel was dog-tired. For the past couple of years, Sergei had been based in Paris, but travelled regularly to America. As his private pilot, Daniel had apartments in both locations, but called neither of them home.

This was his first assignment for Cain and Ben. To talk a reticent spinster into allowing them the use of her house for a no-holds-barred party. He'd checked out the Sex Lies movie on his brother's insistence, and had to admit that the whole premise of the film—illicit sexual liaisons in a country house deep in the English countryside—was erotic.

He'd been surprised when Maxine Goode, the location scout who had approached Miss Hazzard with the proposition, had reported that the house owner hadn't immediately consented. A million was a more than generous amount to tempt the most conservative of women, but apparently she had reservations.

Reservations he was determined to allay during this meeting. In his experience, money could buy anything.

He was staying in a suite, but had decided to come down to the lobby to wait for Miss Hazzard to arrive. She was probably nervous enough, talking to a strange man about using her house for a sex party, and being sent up to his suite alone would make her more uncomfortable. The conversation would be awkward, but not one to have in a public place. He'd told the receptionist he was waiting for someone, had asked her to point Miss Hazzard his direction when she arrived.

Idling the time away watching a beautiful woman was a great distraction.

Sergei never travelled alone, he always had at least three gorgeous women with him as in-flight entertainment, but Daniel was immune to their perfect bodies and flawless looks.

The woman at the reception desk was a different story. She was older, for one, he'd guess mid-thirties, tall, but curvy, not coltish like Sergei's women.

Dark hair lit with chestnut lights tumbled over her shoulders in glorious waves. Her eyes were chocolate colored, fringed with dark lashes, and her mouth was full and soft, perfect for kissing. She wore a black silk dress that hugged her curves and ended at the knees. He'd appreciated her long legs showcased perfectly in fuck-me heels, and wondered how she'd look without the dress. How she'd look naked.

She caught him staring, and to his surprise instead of turning away, stared blatantly back with a challenge in her eyes. A challenge that acknowledged his attraction, and fired it right back at him. Right now, he wished he wasn't waiting for the owner of Hazzard Hall, and could instead approach her.

He wanted to breathe in her scent, hear her voice, touch her lightly tanned skin. Experience her up close and personal.

She had no luggage; perhaps she was meeting someone.

The brunette was speaking to the receptionist, who looked up and scanned the lobby, finally fixing on him. She smiled, nodded and waved him over.

For a moment, Daniel was frozen to the spot. *She's Kathryn Hazzard?* His eyebrows rose in silent query. The receptionist gestured to him again, snapping him out of his stupor and propelling him across the floor to where she stood.

"Miss Hazzard?"

She blinked. Her mouth gaped slightly before she regained control and snapped it shut. "Yes, I'm Kathryn Hazzard." Her English-accented voice was husky.

He held out his hand and she did the same. Her skin was warm and soft. Her grip firm. Their palms rubbed, sparking an electricity that caused his fingers to reflexively curl tighter around hers. "Daniel Hunt."

She didn't pull her hand away. Her full lips parted a fraction as she met his gaze. Close up, there were flecks of gold in her melted-chocolate colored irises, like tiny constellations around the black pupils.

Her subtle scent made his mouth water. "Thank you for meeting me." Daniel released her hand. *Since when was holding a woman's hand enough to make his cock stir?* "We can talk in my suite."

"Fine." She tucked a lock of hair behind her ear revealing a discreet red-gold earring in the form of a star with a tiny pearl dead center. Expensive and antique, the earrings were her only adornment. A crazy desire to bring his mouth to the curve of her neck below them struck from nowhere, the urge to taste her skin with his tongue, abrade it with his teeth.

Instead, he turned to the receptionist. "I'd like room-service to deliver my order to my suite now, please."

"Of course, Mr. Hunt."

"This way." He led Kathryn Hazzard to the elevator.

*****

Daniel Hunt didn't speak until room service had arrived and been set up on the table in the sumptuous suite. "Coffee? Tea?"

She shook her head.

He poured himself coffee, and gestured to the matching sofas in the seating area. "Make yourself comfortable, Miss Hazzard."

"Call me Kathryn." What were the odds that the man she'd been flirting with in the lobby was the one she'd come here to meet? She licked her dry lips and tried to still the flutter of nerves. Her palm still tingled from his touch and she rubbed it over her thigh. The way he looked at her—steady and watchful, made her painfully aware of him. Every inch of her body was super-sensitized under his regard.

When she crossed her legs, his gaze flickered to her legs with a flash of heat he didn't even try to hide.

She pressed her thighs together and tried to quench the feelings stirring within. *This is business.*

"Kathryn." His American drawl made the tiny hairs on the back of her neck stand up. "And you must call me Daniel."

He smiled, deep, sexy as hell dimples appearing as deep grooves in his cheeks. His hair was parted at the side, and a lock of hair tumbled, almost obscuring a dark eyebrow, as though he'd been raking his hands through it.

How might it feel beneath her fingers? She couldn't seem to look away from the sensuous curve of his mouth. Her fingers urged to touch him. To get close and breathe in his scent. Her nipples stiffened inside the lace of her bra at the thought. She hadn't felt like this for years, had she ever in fact been so turned on by a man that her body's response had been so urgent?

And he hadn't done anything but smile at her.

"Have you thought more about my offer?"

"I've thought of it constantly," she answered honestly. "It's been causing me sleepless nights." A rueful smile teased her lips. "It's one hell of an offer."

"Yet you haven't decided to take it?" Even his voice was distracting, deep, drawly, and tingle inducing. *Get a grip*.

She ran her tongue up behind her front teeth. Tried to look businesslike. "There are issues. Elements of your proposition that concern me."

He took two bound sheaves of paper from the coffee table, and passed one to her. "Let's go through them, one by one. I'm sure I can allay whatever fears you have."

His clients were so desperate for her house he'd flown in for this meeting. Money seemed to be no obstacle—his clients must be so rich they did whatever their hearts desired. She forced down resentment at the thought of money without responsibilities.

Their situations were so different, he couldn't understand her concerns, but she owed it to herself—to Hazzard—to listen. She nodded.

"I don't know what sort of people your clients are…" Her gaze avoided his. "I don't know anything about them."

"You suspect they might be drug dealers or mafia?" Daniel softened his words with a smile. "I can assure you that my clients are decent men who have come by their riches honestly. Off the record, my clients are the owners of Bigtalk."

Her eyes widened—everyone in the world was aware of Bigtalk at the moment.

"With their newly acquired riches, my brother and his business partner have decided to indulge a few of their fantasies."

"England is a long way to come for a sexual experience."

"Yes. It is. But they're not just after a sexual experience. Both of them are huge fans of the Sex Lies movie. They wanted everything to be the same. Full-length black cloaks, masks, black-clad servants, and a masked keyboard player playing atmospheric music on a synthesizer in the corner of the drawing-room. Half-naked, gorgeous women stalking around, taking control. Fantasy made real. No holding back."

"Surely it would be easier to recreate the house in America?"

"It would be. I tried to talk them into that. My clients are rich enough to recreate the house used in Sex Lies in any country they choose, but they're purists who aren't prepared to compromise. They want to walk through the front door of your house in the dark of night just as the character in the film did. They want the same experience, or as close as they can get to it."

"But they know that the people…that they were actors, right?" The thought of prostitutes in her home, there for his clients' use was abhorrent. "That it wasn't real?"

"Of course." He drained his coffee and placed it on the table. "My clients," he sighed. "What you have to understand about them is that they are inexperienced in these matters. They want to fulfill a fantasy—one they haven't had the opportunity to indulge before now. It's not about the fucking, it's about role-playing."

"So—the other guests—are they friends?"

"No. The other guests are members of an exclusive sex club, which operates in a number of countries worldwide. They are all of high net worth, and enjoy the lifestyle. Many of them are in the public eye, and discretion is paramount." He flicked open the report. "Each guest will be invited, and will have to give a password to be allowed admittance. There will be a confidentiality agreement signed by all to protect your privacy, and that of each guest."

"They'll be masked?"

"As in the film, yes."

"My furniture..." She couldn't bring herself to talk about how she'd feel about strangers screwing on her dining room table.

"What happened to your furniture during Sex Lies?"

The film and this situation couldn't be compared. The actors had been acting—simulating sex, rather than actually doing it. And her furniture hadn't been deemed suitable anyway; the director had wanted a gothic feel to the house's interior. "They replaced it."

"As we would." He flicked another page with long, tanned fingers. "Maxine has been tasked with recreating the interior exactly. We will pay to remove your house contents into storage, and replace them with furniture from the same prop company that furnished the house for the film."

He turned over another page. "A thorough security

check will be run on each guest before they make the guest list, and everyone who attends the evening will have to submit to a health screening."

Kathryn's eyes widened.

Daniel elaborated. "All the usual health-checks and prophylactics will be seen to and documentation provided."

"I think I need a glass of water." Talking about the details so dispassionately with him was making her hot and bothered. Kathryn shifted on the sofa as Daniel rose and poured her a glass of sparkling water from the bar in the corner of the lounge.

He walked back, and handed it over.

"Thank you." She took a sip then placed the tall glass on the coffee table.

"Everyone who attends will have to satisfy these demands," he explained. "Even the serving staff. That may sound excessive, but these events are spontaneous—if someone wants to play, even if they hadn't previously intended to, they have to be screened in case things take an unexpected turn."

"Fine." She clasped her hands together in her lap, and tried not to wonder if Daniel intended to play, or might be influenced by 'an unexpected turn of events.'

"I don't intend to play." The damned man could add telepathy to his list of considerable assets. "I'll be attending to make sure things run smoothly, not to participate in the evening's delights."

"But you'll be checked anyway, just in case." She wished she could call back the suggestive words the moment they left her mouth.

His eyes scorched her with the banked heat evident in their depths.

"Of course."

Kathryn lifted the hair from the back of her neck in an attempt to cool down. "I can't believe I'm considering this."

His stare was unwavering. His forehead wrinkled when his brows rose. "You are still not happy about it?"

"How can I be? Hazzard is my home, my sanctuary…"

He leaned forward. Looked at her mouth. And molten heat flashed from her stomach to between her legs. "Two million," he murmured in a deep voice. "And you agree tonight."

Chapter Three

Shock thundered through Kathryn at his words. *Two million? Did he really say...*

"Two million?" A whispered squeak. "You just doubled it?"

"I want your house." His gaze sizzled with heat he didn't even try to hide. "But this is a time-sensitive offer, Kathryn." He eased back in the chair. "You have until midnight to say yes or no. After that, the offer expires."

She should be considering his proposition rationally, but was flustered now he'd doubled the fee. "I...I should go home. Think about your offer. I can call you."

She couldn't think straight while he looked at her like that, as though he wanted to eat her alive. She'd always prided herself on her ability to keep her feelings hidden, but Daniel's bombshell had exploded around her, blowing her composure to pieces. In the wreckage, shards of fantasy scenarios including her and him—in bed or out of it, and lots of hot, sweaty sex littered the battleground of her mind.

She twisted her hands together. She needed to talk to Max, needed to run over the pros and cons of setting up her house as a fantasy sex club. "I've never even been to a sex club. I don't know what to expect…what I'm letting myself in for."

"Sitting at home considering my offer isn't going to advance things any, is it? You need to see a club in action. Knowledge is power, yes?" Daniel picked up the phone and called reception.

Kathryn's head swam as he booked her a suite next door to his, and asked the concierge to bring the key to them. When the call was over he hung up and walked over. He extended a hand, and pulled her up. His hand lingered on her upper arm as he looked down into her face. Kathryn rarely had to look up into a man's face. At almost six feet, with a penchant for heels, she more often than not looked down on men.

Daniel topped her by a good two inches.

"I understand your reticence." His deep voice made the hairs on her arms rise. "And of course it isn't fair to expect your agreement if you haven't ever visited a club where sex is the primary focus. Many of the guests for the evening at your house are members of Lucien Knight's Gateway Club here in London. I'll organize a visit for us there this evening."

She'd always been intrigued by the idea of visiting a club, but with this man… "I couldn't—"

"Couldn't what, Kathryn? Experience for yourself just how these places operate? Perhaps you'd feel more comfortable if you brought a lover along. Is there someone you can call to accompany us?"

Admitting that she was currently unattached had a touch of TMI about it. Had the potential to shift their conversation into dangerous territory. *Stop being such a wuss.* "No, I don't."

One perfect black brow arched. His slow smile cut deep dimples into his cheeks again, making him look like a seductive pirate. Instead of feeling nervous, a tingle of wicked anticipation raced her spine. "You're single?"

"Currently, yes." She'd been proposed to a couple of times—had even considered one of them for a while before the thought of tying herself to one man forever had made her pull back and reconsider. She'd always had a wild side—a need to fully explore her sexual preferences that had held her back from the ultimate commitment. The men her father approved of as suitable partners were so traditional in the sack they totally left her cold.

Like a perfect bitch, she had a pedigree to die for, the sole remaining member of an old, aristocratic family, and was damned to be chased around by men either wanting the cachet of being married to a Hazzard, or ones who thought that the name and house signified that there must be a pile of money stacked up in a bank vault to match.

Short term hook-ups far from home on her brief holidays from work had so far been the perfect answer. She'd romanced men in Paris, in Rome, and in Monte Carlo. Men unaware of her pedigree, unaware of her past. While her father had been alive it had been essential to keep any trace of scandal from tainting the family name, or ending up on the front pages of the tabloids. At work, she was merely one of many—valued for her expertise, not her name. She'd always guarded her privacy there—no-one even knew the double life she led.

But Dad was dead now. And this club must be discreet, she'd never heard of it, or of Lucien Knight. And anyway, this was business, not pleasure—it would be best not to confuse the two.

"I'm going to need some clothes," she said. "What's the dress code for the Gateway Club?" She didn't want to enter the club wearing a corset or something, but at the same time she didn't want to stand out either.

"People wear whatever they want," Daniel said. "There are changing rooms available so people can dress to attract if they desire. I'll leave that decision up to you. I will try to organize a tour from Lucien or his representative, so I guess you might want to wear something less revealing for that. There is plenty of time before we leave to choose either one outfit or two."

Kathryn pulled in a swift breath.

A knock on the door heralded the arrival of a hotel employee with the key to her suite.

Kathryn picked up her bag.

"Shall we meet for dinner?" Daniel asked.

"I'll think I'll just grab something in my suite." *Retreat, regroup, get the mask back on.*

"Okay, so I'll call for you at nine and we'll head out." Daniel placed his hand on the curve of her back as he walked her to the door. He brushed her cheek with his mouth in an innocuous kiss that heated her blood.

She breathed in his expensive, musky scent. "I'm looking forward to it."

And from the heat banked in his eyes, the sentiment was definitely reciprocated.

*****

Daniel spent the remainder of the afternoon on the telephone. He organized the visit to The Gateway Club, and skyped Christopher Atleigh, the new business manager he'd appointed to deal with Cain and Ben's business affairs. Christopher had an online conference with one of the UK's top business magazines who were keen to feature Cain and Ben on their cover together with a detailed article about their company's product. He called Cain, but his brother once again had his phone off, so he left a brief message saying he was going out but would check in later.

Pushing thoughts of the enticing Kathryn Hazzard from his mind was proving difficult. She was an intriguing mix of sexy and confident. Her voice reminded him of an actress in one of those English Historical TV series and had made his cock stir, even when she was talking business.

When she saw him in the lobby, the way she looked at him, straight and sure, telegraphed that she was a woman at ease with her sexuality—one who knew what she wanted and had no compunction going after it. On discovering he was the man she'd come here to meet that had changed. She avoided looking at him, and when she did, her cheeks flushed with color. She was single. And interested—even if she didn't want to be—at the thought of this evening.

He'd spent the last few months flying Sergei around the world. Being a free agent, he'd taken time along the way to slake his body's thirsts with willing partners, but had become jaded and bored by the last few women he'd slept with. Sure they were gorgeous, feminine, and experienced.

But they lacked a certain something. And Kathryn Hazzard intrigued him.

At one minute past nine, he knocked on the door to her suite. A moment later, it swung open. She wore a black tuxedo jacket, and a glittery silver miniskirt that clung to every curve. Her legs seemed to go on forever, and the heels, higher than the ones she'd worn earlier, brought her eyes up to his mouth. The tux jacket was fastened by a single button mid-torso. Underneath it, she wore precisely nothing. A long silver chain with a diamond circlet hung above the curve of her breasts.

Her dark chocolate hair was caught up in a topknot, and curling tendrils brushed her shoulders. With every inhale Daniel breathed in the warm spicy scent of her perfume. Small diamond studs glittered at her earlobes.

"You look spectacular." She wore drop dead sexy effortlessly. He wanted to trail his lips down the curve of her neck, lick her breastbone, flick his tongue over the erect nipples he felt sure he'd find if he nudged the jacket lapel aside. Daniel rubbed the back of his neck. "Let's go."

*****

The Gateway Club was nothing like Kathryn expected. The outside of the club was low rise and modern, its exterior all smoked glass. Daniel ushered them past the queue of waiting club goers and gave his name to the doorman, who nodded and opened the door wide into the reception area. "Just go straight through into the club, Mr. Hunt," he said, before speaking into the tiny microphone that snaked from his ear. "They're expecting you."

They passed through the subtly lit reception to the double doors that led into the club's interior. She'd been in many London nightclubs, their darkened interiors hid a great deal, and she knew that in the cold light of day they often looked worn and seedy. Not this club though. Everything about it screamed money, from the opulent aubergine velvet of the private seating nooks that spanned the room, to the gilt and crystal chandeliers. Her ears were assaulted by the music, heavy bass reverberated through her chest and the sexy slide of the melody ratcheted excitement up a notch. The dance floor was full of people. To a casual glance, they seemed just like regular club goers. Daniel took her hand and brought her across the room to a couple of empty high metal stools at the bar.

Kathryn sat, crossing her legs. "Are we meeting someone?"

Daniel shook his head. "Lucien is out of the country, and his assistant suggested that we explore the club on our own. Enjoy ourselves. Would you like a long, slow comfortable screw against the wall?" Daniel's smile was lethal. His gaze flickered to the edge of the bar, where a tall redhead was getting exactly that. Well, not exactly that, there seemed nothing long, slow or comfortable about it.

She wore a red bustier, tightly laced, with slits strategically placed to allow her pink nipples to protrude through the fabric. Black fishnet stockings were attached to suspenders. Her partner gripped the creamy globes of her bottom, and her legs were wrapped around his waist. His leather jeans were around his knees. Kathryn felt heat flood her as his firm buttocks flexed as he slammed himself into the redhead again and again.

Her head was thrown back, and her mouth opened on a scream of bliss that couldn't be heard above the sound of the music. "There's nothing slow about that," Kathryn murmured.

Daniel placed his hand high on her thigh, and with the other called the bartender over. "A long, slow, comfortable screw against the wall for the lady, and a glass of Maximum Extra Anejo over ice."

The bartender smiled. "Good choice, sir." He picked a glass bottle of a caramel colored liquid from the shelf behind the bar and poured it, then assembled the ingredients for Kathryn's cocktail.

"Is that whisky?" The color didn't seem right.

"Aged rum." His fingers moved against her skin, and the urge to uncross her legs, to encourage them to move higher was almost overwhelming. "There are private rooms upstairs."

The bartender put her drink down before her with a flourish.

"So this is a long, comfortable screw against the wall." She took a sip of the orange liquid, and looked at Daniel.

He ran a finger around his collar and reached for his drink. "I could listen to your voice all day."

Amused, Kathryn smiled. More than once she'd been told men found her voice sexy. "Saying what?" she teased.

"Saying goddamn anything. You could even make a shopping list sound sexy." He drank a long swallow and stood. "Are you ready for the tour?"

Nerves clenched in Kathryn's stomach. She needed to see everything. Needed to evaluate what hosting a sex party entailed. As repellent as the thought of having a crowd of strangers in her house was, she had to consider it and make a quick decision. In a little over three hours his offer would expire. "Okay." She stood too.

She walked ahead of him up the staircase that led to the upper level. A man, stripped to the waist passed them on the stairs, blatantly staring at the wide expanse of skin between the lapels of her tuxedo jacket. The stranger smiled, and licked his lips.

Daniel's arm curved around her waist as he stepped up behind her.

His fingers slipped beneath the tuxedo jacket and splayed across her stomach. Heat radiated from the hard, strong body that pressed against hers. "Mine," he growled, staring the other man down. As if to prove a point, he stroked his hand over her hair, pushed it aside and ran his lips down her neck.

The stranger nodded and carried on walking.

Kathryn's heart raced. She turned, and as Daniel was one step below her, found his eyes staring into hers. "I'm not yours," she whispered, even as her traitorous body denied her words. His hands were still on her naked flesh, stroking her waist under the jacket.

Daniel stared at her mouth. "Not yet."

She bit her bottom lip, desperate to quench the bewildering desire to feel his hands on her breasts. "We're here on business."

"Did you want me to give you to him?" He withdrew a hand and rubbed her bottom lip with his thumb. On a scale of one to ten it was a one compared to the blatant sexuality displayed wherever she looked, but still had the potency to make her shiver.

The more time she spent with him, the stronger the attraction grew. "Of course not." She swallowed as a flash of heat rushed into her face.

With just a look, he exuded such powerful sensuality she wished she didn't have any business to discuss with him. That they were strangers, as they had been the first moment she'd seen him. That first moment in the hotel foyer she'd instantly sized him up as a potential fuck buddy and pictured them in bed.

"Relax, Kathryn," he whispered. "Nothing will happen unless you want it to." Releasing her, he stepped to her side. The sound of the music was quieter up in the corridor. There were a few rooms, some with doors open, some closed.

Daniel stopped at the first door. "From what I

remember, this room is for those into being caged and whipped. A closed door signifies that the participants don't want to be disturbed."

Kathryn swallowed.

"We can check it later, if the door is open." Daniel walked to the next room. The door was closed, but had a glass panel in it. "Lucien's steam room. We'd need to get naked before going in here." He gestured to a smaller changing room next to it. "Want to get steamy?"

Through the window Kathryn vaguely made out naked bodies, there must be four or five, though it was difficult to tell in the steam rising around them, and the fact that they all seemed to be entangled. One beautiful woman knelt on the slatted wooden boards, her mouth around a man's cock as another man stood behind her, gripping her hips as he drove into her again and again. On the floor under her, another woman was sliding her hands and her mouth over the woman's breasts.

"I...I think we should check the next room," Kathryn croaked.

Daniel's laugh skittered over her nerve endings. "We don't have to. If you're uncomfortable, we can leave."

What was she, woman or mouse? Kathryn pressed her lips together. She was no timid virgin. Watching the woman, she'd imagined what it must feel like to be the center of such dedicated attention, and despite the fact that she'd never been attracted to the thought of threesomes, or foursomes, for that matter, she'd felt the unmistakable stirrings of arousal.

She pushed past Daniel and walked into the next room.

The room was dominated by a large central table

covered in sheepskin. A group of men and women stood around it, watching as an Asian woman with long hair that skimmed the top of her naked ass sprayed another two prone women with a can of whipped cream. She covered their mons with the soft foam, their belly buttons and nipples, then carefully took strawberries from a container by her side, and decorated them.

When she was finished, she stood back, threw her arms open wide and smiled as the audience dived in, licking and biting the cream and fruit from the women's bodies.

Kathryn held her breath at the sight of such abandon. The bodies on display were perfect—all different, but all sleek and toned. For a moment, she wondered where all the normal people partied—but she guessed that those with enough money and an interest in getting naked were also the type to spend money maintaining their bodies.

She was thirty-five, not twenty. Her body had never given birth, and her stomach was taut and tight, but gravity and time had stolen the perkiness from her breasts. She wasn't as body-confident as these people. And the thought of a stranger doing to her what these strangers were doing to the women on the table…

She turned away.

"Let's go downstairs. There's a movie theatre down at the back, but there won't be anything like that at your house, so we don't need to see that unless you want to."

She'd had enough. Didn't think she could enter another room; could see more vivid images of people screwing. Her senses were overloaded, fried. "I've seen enough."

Downstairs, Daniel led her past the private booths. In the first a naked woman lay on her back on the aubergine velvet. Back arched in ecstasy, her legs were bent and her high heels spiked into the walls. The hands of her enthusiastic partner clutched around her milky thighs. His head moved between her outspread legs; and his tongue plunged into her vagina. A bead of moisture glistened on the tip of his engorged cock as he drove the woman toward her orgasm. Kathryn had thought she couldn't take any more, but the way the woman was squeezing her breasts fired Kathryn's blood, made her long to do the same to her own.

The woman moaned.

Her partner slid up her body, fastened his mouth around her breast, and jerked her up onto his lap. His cock slid inside her easily, and the woman gripped his shoulders and pushed her breasts into his face.

"You're staring," Daniel's deep voice whispered in her ear. He touched the side of her face, ran his fingers down her throat then back up to turn her face to his. He was so close his breath feathered against her parted lips. "It turns you on, doesn't it, Kathryn?" Her answer must have been evident in her eyes, for without waiting for a reply he pressed his mouth to hers.

They were here on business. Getting involved with Daniel Hunt was a bad idea. And yet, when his mouth claimed hers, and his hand touched her skin, she couldn't resist any longer. Her lips parted, and he probed her mouth in a passionate kiss that set her nerve endings alight. His hand cupped her face.

She turned in his arms and pressed her body to his. Slipping her arms around his neck she gave herself totally to the sensation of his hard chest against her. His erection pressed into her stomach, arousing her to an unbearable pitch.

"Come on." His voice was rough. Taking her hand, he tugged her into a nearby vacant booth. "I need your tits in my hands so bad I can't wait."

Chapter Four

His words inflamed her, made her nipples, naked under the tuxedo's silk lining, throb and tighten. Wordlessly, she followed him into the booth. Daniel sat, and she stood before him, her parted legs bracketing his. He jerked open his tie, and undid his top button, all the time watching her with heat simmering in his emerald eyes.

The lights were dim in the secluded booth, but if the other partygoers chose, they could see exactly what was going on—could watch Daniel and her having sex. The thought should have given her pause, but instead her panties dampened.

Daniel undid the single button holding her jacket closed, and parted it to reveal her to his eyes. "Beautiful." His hands slid up her torso and cupped each breast. "You're totally fucking beautiful." He leaned forward, and took one stiffened nipple into his mouth.

Kathryn gasped at the sensation of his tongue flicking over her flesh. A cord of want tightened from the point of contact, snaking down through her body to her clit. Watching had been arousing, but actually having Daniel's mouth on her went far beyond. She looked down at his dark head moving on her pale skin and shivered. He was beautiful too. She needed more. Needed to be closer.

His mouth released her for a moment, and he rested the side of his head over her thundering heartbeat. "Ah, there it is." He reached out for a tiny button next to the light switch, and turned it, dimming the faint light to almost black. "I don't want anyone watching what I'm doing to you," he growled. "You're mine."

His hands slipped to her bottom, eased under the hem of her tiny skirt, and brushed the soft silk of her panties. Then he turned his attentions to her other breast.

She gripped his shoulders. Her head fell back. Her legs trembled.

A few hours ago, she hadn't even known this man, but now all she wanted was to touch his skin, explore every inch of him, feel his cock thrust inside her. Maybe it was just the abstinence forced on her over the past few months looking after her father during his illness combined with the heady drugging influence of being in a place where everything was allowed, nothing was taboo. His fingers slipped the edge of her panties aside, and one long finger rubbed against her clit.

She moaned.

As if realizing that her shaking legs wouldn't be able to support her when he quested further, Daniel pulled her close, so her knees rested on the plush aubergine velvet, bracketing him. "Better?"

"Better," she echoed.

His thumb moved over her clit then he slid two fingers into her. "You're so damned wet."

She reached down to stroke over the hard bulge in his pants but he shook his head. "Not here. Not now. Just let me touch you. Let me make you come." Everything paled into insignificance with the insistent rub of his thumb, the curling of his fingers. She met his mouth hungrily, reveling in sensation as his tongue thrust into her, echoing the frantic movement of his fingers. She'd never felt such bone deep arousal, such desire, and when his hand curved around her ass, and forced her forward, the pressure built to unbearable.

She couldn't hold on…couldn't…

His mouth moved to her neck, he sucked on her skin and nibbled.

Her body was like a firework, touch paper licked by a flame, causing a flash that raced through her body. She did as he asked, and came harder than she'd ever had in her entire life.

*****

Daniel snaked both arms around Kathryn and held her tight as she slumped against him. His heart was pounding, and his breathing fast. Despite the fact that his body hadn't had its own release, satisfaction swelled deep inside. Together with the urge to protect.

He smoothed a hand over her back. Breathed in the scent that rose from her hair, and her fevered body. His fiercely proprietorial reaction to the guy flirting with her on the stairs had taken him by surprise. They'd come to the Gateway for business, but the moment she'd murmured the name of the cocktail at the bar in her husky accented tones, his body has known this evening couldn't end without him making her come.

And she just had. So spectacularly it astounded him.

The sights and sounds of the other club goers, the blatant sexuality that assaulted both of them as they travelled from room to room had been arousing. Despite the obvious charms of the other women, it had been Kathryn who held his attention. Kathryn he wanted to taste, to touch, to fuck.

She came from a different world—hell, she'd probably never worked a day in her life. Like a princess in an ivory tower she'd been sheltered by her family, more than likely basked in her parents' love. He and Cain were different. When their parents divorced, his mother had left them behind. Guilt had driven her to pay their way through college, but she'd never asked them out to visit. Her wealthy new husband hadn't signed up for a package deal. Intrigued and fascinated as he was by the beautiful Kathryn Hazzard, a relationship between them couldn't possibly work.

And he didn't do relationships anyway—not lasting ones. He'd trusted a woman once, but never again.

His arms tightened around her as she kissed the side of his jaw, and his cock jerked. *Less than an hour to go before that crazy deadline.* He'd been impatient, determined to sway her decision about using her house in his favor, so much so he'd added another million into the mix, and tacked on a time limit to force the issue. He was due to fly out in a few hours, and needed to tie up the agreement before he left.

Now, he didn't want her capitulation, because then he'd have no excuse to stay. And the only thing he wanted to tie up was her gorgeous body to his bed.

He wasn't ready to let her go yet.

Daniel angled his face to hers. Kissed her soft lips. "Let's go."

They were on their way to the car when a screeching of brakes and the sickening crunch of metal shattered the stillness of the night. Daniel swung around to see two cars that had collided at an intersection nearby. A cloud of steam hissed into the air from the point of impact, and fractured metal was strewn across the road. One of them had shot the lights and crashed into the other, slamming into the driver's side.

Before he could even reach into his pocket for his cellphone to call for an ambulance, Kathryn was running straight for them.

"Kathryn!" He took off after her.

"Call for an ambulance," she shouted as she went to the first driver. She reached into the car, talking to the driver, then waved Daniel over. "Stay with this man while I check the other driver." She glanced under the car, then dashed to the other vehicle.

Daniel took out his phone and made the call.

Kathryn was talking to the second driver, assessing her injuries. Her hands went into the car, turning off the ignition. She held the driver's head, telling her not to move.

"It's imperative that her neck is supported," she said to Daniel. "The other driver seems to be stunned but uninjured. He needs to stay in his car."

"Shouldn't we get them away from the vehicles?"

"Both engines are off, and the fuel tanks haven't been ruptured, I checked," Kathryn said. "There's a hospital nearby that runs an ambulance service, paramedics should be here in a moment."

"I'll go back into the club, see if I can find a doctor..."

Kathryn shook her head. "No need. I'm a doctor."

She's a doctor? "I...I thought..."

A wry smile was on Kathryn's face. "You thought I was a rich bitch living off Daddy's money?" Her words summed up what he had thought so precisely Daniel felt his face heat. He hadn't even considered that Kathryn might have a job, never mind a profession.

"I trained as a doctor and was working in an accident and emergency department of a large hospital when my father got sick. I needed to take time off to care for him, and then after he died…well, I've been busy with taxes and trying to rescue our home." The faint sound of sirens pierced the air.

"Don't worry, the ambulance is almost here," she said to the distressed woman whose head she still supported in her hands. "Just stay calm."

*****

Even as she worked with the paramedics, putting a neck collar onto the injured passenger, and observing them strapping the woman onto a back-board before loading her in the ambulance, Kathryn was acutely aware of Daniel in the background. He stood to the side, watching everything that was going on.

It had been a year since she had been in the cut and thrust of things, and she missed it. Her job had given meaning to her life—there she was just a doctor, a professional doing a job. She missed both the satisfaction she received for a job well done, and the camaraderie of working with a team. When Dad got sick, she'd thought the leaving would be temporary, but now…well, she couldn't fathom how to get back to the person she'd been a year ago. Someone without the responsibility of saving her home hanging around her neck like a dead weight pulling her under.

She stood in the middle of the road, and watched the ambulance grow smaller as it sped away.

Daniel walked up and slipped his arm through hers.

"You okay?"

She nodded.

"It's almost eleven."

Her back stiffened. The events of the past half-hour had forced thoughts of the decision she had yet to make from her mind, and she still didn't know what to say, which way to jump. The feeling of being pressured, or having to make an important decision—a final decision, tightened her chest and made it difficult to breathe. She needed the money. The house needed the money. She rolled her top lip inward and pressed down.

Daniel's hand caressed her upper arm. "Have you decided?"

She shook her head. Crossed her arms. Glanced at the thin gold watch on her wrist. "I still have an hour."

"Let's go back to the hotel." He hailed a passing cab.

On leaving the club, Kathryn had been wild, had been held tight in the grip of desire. The accident had changed that. She'd been given a moment of respite by having to focus on the injured driver. Thought had overtaken instinct, and given her pause. What was she doing? Diving straight into a sexual relationship with Daniel Hunt, on reflection, was a very bad idea.

Her thigh was against his in the taxi, and his body heat seeped into her chilled leg. She glanced at his profile, wondering about the man who had managed to make her so desperate that she'd climbed onto his lap and encouraged him to bring her to orgasm in a room full of people.

She angled her thigh away and stared from the window.

The drive to the hotel was a short one, and in mere moments they were entering the lobby and claiming the keys to their suites. In the elevator, he made no move to touch her, a fact that churned up conflicting emotions. On one hand, she was glad to have some distance, some perspective. On the other—she wanted nothing more than to avoid reality in the fevered embrace of his arms.

"Come for a nightcap?" he asked.

"I don't know." She looked down at her clothes, noting for the first time the smear of blood on her jacket, the grime and dust from contact with the crushed metal. "I should shower."

"Bring your bag into my room. You can shower and change. We can talk."

His gaze was steady. His words weren't suggestive, and the way he delivered them wasn't flirtatious. Passion seemed to have cooled for them both. And they did need to talk.

"Okay." She opened her door, snatched up the overnight bag she'd bought that afternoon, and joined him in his room.

Chapter Five

Daniel poured himself a shot of rum, added ice, and gazed out of the window at the darkened city as she showered. In a city like London, the night was never really dark; lights glittered in the blackness, and the streets were filled with revelers. It was almost midnight. He wanted closure on this matter of Hazzard Hall. Wanted to wrap up the entire package, and get on the plane back to America with a signed contract in his pocket.

But had no desire to run away from Kathryn Hazzard.

Maybe they could spend more time together. He had a week to kill before Cain was back from his vacation, and he sure wasn't ready to walk away from her yet.

"Hi." Kathryn's voice was soft.

He turned from the window to see her standing in the doorway of the bathroom, dressed in a pair of jeans, a white T-shirt and a hint of vulnerability in the depths of her eyes.

He poured her a glass of champagne, and walked across the room to her. "You were amazing back there."

Her mouth curved into a smile. "In the club?"

He shook his head. "At the accident. You knew exactly what to do."

"Practice." She blew off his words, as if they were of no importance. "When manning a busy accident and emergency department you have to be ready for anything. She was damned lucky, you know. If the car had hit six inches up, her legs would have been pinned."

The women he'd known wouldn't have even attempted to help, would have stood back and let someone else do it. Sure, she was trained for it, but she was different, very different. She'd dived straight in, hadn't been remotely worried about the dirt and blood that stained her new clothing. Her focus had been one hundred percent on the injured. He'd never expected to feel both desire and admiration for the same person.

He checked his watch. "Midnight. Whatever your decision, Kathryn, I want you to stay with me tonight."

She gazed at his mouth. "I have made my decision." She swallowed a mouthful of champagne. "I can't turn down that sort of money. I accept." She held up her glass and clinked it against his. "Hazzard is yours for one night."

He stepped close, and brushed his lips against hers in a kiss so gentle it surprised the hell out of him. "Both Hazzards?" One night wouldn't be enough, but they had to start somewhere.

A soft exhale puffed from her, and the tips of her fingers touched his face. "Daniel..." she whispered in a way that made him instantly hard. "I...this is all going too fast."

"You want me, Kathryn," he said against her mouth. "I want you. There's no denying it. And for more than just one night. I want to taste every single inch of you. Want you gripping my back with your fingers, taking my cock deep into your mouth and your body."

She sucked in a sharp breath, her eyes widened, and darkened to almost black. His words had shocked, but also aroused her.

"I can change my plans. Put off going back to the States for a while. How long has it been since you had a vacation?" He slipped a hand under her T-shirt. She smelled faintly of soap, had removed her makeup in the shower. Tiny wrinkles fanned from the corners of her eyes. Laugh lines. When had she last laughed?

"A couple of years," she admitted. "Before my father became ill."

"So we get on a plane, leave behind your house, your money worries, and escape to the sun for a week. Just the two of us—alone in paradise. We can fuck all day and all night. Swim in the ocean. Recharge our minds and our spirits. I sure as hell need it, and I think you do too."

"I can't do that." Her tongue swiped across her bottom lip. "A relationship…"

"I'm not talking a lifetime. I'm talking about a tiny slice out of our lives. A stolen week. A chance to get to know each other better."

She rubbed the spot below her ear. "And fuck."

"Yes."

Her head tilted to the side. Her fingers smoothed over his chest, curled around his tie. "All day and all night."

"It'll be good." His damn voice was close to a growl as her fingers undid his tie.

"I was going to hide in my room, and sleep," she said. "After the accident, I had no intention of having sex with you." She slipped off his tie and undid his top button. He held his breath as she trailed her lips across his jawline. "My body seems to have other ideas though."

"Well, damn well listen to your body. It knows what it wants." His control shattered as she undid another button. "It wants to be lying under me, arching in fucking bliss as I eat you."

*****

The decision to pimp out her house had been made, and instead of the anticipated feeling of despair, Kathryn's mind cleared, seeing only the positives that two million dollars could bring. Her worries dissolved, leaving her free to focus all her attentions on the man before her. She liked touching him. Found his words and his reserve as she'd stripped off his tie empowering and arousing. But when he turned on the heat, he totally blew her away.

He stripped her T-shirt and jeans off so rapidly she was breathless. His strong arm slid around her, hand splaying against the curve of her back; he jerked her close and claimed her mouth. His tongue traced her teeth, dueled with hers as his other hand covered her naked breast.

Her nipples were hard, and heat pooled in her stomach.

"I barely know you." It had only been a few short hours since they'd met—never before had she got so hot, so heavy in such a short time with anyone. "We're practically strangers."

Daniel stared into her eyes. "We *were* strangers. I agree, this thing between us is happening fast, but I'm not a stranger to you, Kathryn. Not any longer. We can be lovers."

She looked down at the large, tanned hand cupping her breast. "Just for one night."

"Longer." Daniel growled. "I'm single, so are you. I

suggest we become lovers until either of us wants out."

Heat flared, hot and urgent at his words. She wanted him. Denying herself would probably be smart, but being smart was overrated, especially if it meant walking away from this man.

She ripped open his shirt and forced it from his shoulders.

He pulled back. "Wait." His shirtsleeves were around his wrists, unable to fall free as the cuff buttons were still fastened.

"I like you confined." She lowered her head and kissed his collarbone. He had a beautiful body—his chest was hard and sculpted with muscles that would put Michelangelo's David to shame. A faint trace of dark hair arrowed beneath the waist of his tailored pants, and under it his lean stomach rippled with a taut eight-pack of muscle. He must work out. *A lot.*

"Too fucking bad," he growled, working the cuff buttons free. "I want my hands on you." He sucked one erect nipple, flicking the other between his fingers.

Her breathing was rapid, frantic. She wanted all of him with an overwhelming urgency. Shaking hands unbuckled his belt, and undid the button of his fly, then, unable to take her time, she shoved her hands down the front of his pants, and curled her fingers around his length.

Jesus, he's big.

She wanted to see. Was desperate to taste.

"Shit, I wish we were far away from everywhere so I could make you scream without the possibility of scandalizing the entire hotel," Daniel said.

"I'm not a screamer."

Daniel bit her ear lobe, and whispered in her ear. "Oh

yes you are, you just don't know it yet." He moved—causing her hand to release his cock. Then, with a wicked grin, he hooked his fingers into the sides of her panties and pushed them down.

Kathryn's breath stalled in her throat as his gaze travelled slowly, blatantly, over her bare breasts, to the apex of her thighs. Under his scorching gaze, heat pooled in her stomach, and she felt dampness between her thighs.

"You're beautiful." He unzipped his pants and shoved them and his boxers off. His cock sprang free, jutting toward her.

She reached for him, but he shook his head. "Not yet."

His large palm was warm against her stomach. Then, in slow, deliberate strokes, he caressed her breasts, her hips, her ass. "Turn around," he ordered in a husky murmur. "Let me see you."

Her skin flushed at the desire in his voice. Exposed before him, under such intense scrutiny, she couldn't help thinking of the women in the club, the women with perfect bodies. She wasn't a porn star or a Hollywood actress, just a woman with a regular body—one that never saw the gym. "There's not much to see." The fashion for big-butt curves was empowering for those who actually had them, but hers had always been unremarkable.

"See this?" Daniel curled his hand around his cock. "Can you see how much I want you, Kathryn? How much you turn me on?" She still didn't move, so he did instead.

His thumbs traced both sides of her spine. His fingers splayed across her back. Travelling lower, they smoothed over the curve of her hips—gripped her butt. He made a sound. Half groan, half growl.

An unmistakable sound of desire that empowered her, banished the last hint of awkwardness.

He pulled her against his erection and cupped her breasts. His breath feathered against her ear. His teeth nipped her earlobe, then he pushed her hair aside with his face, and traced the sensitive skin from ear to shoulder.

"I want to be in you." His cock twitched between her butt cheeks. "I want to be in you so bad I ache."

She ground her hips back. She'd been on the pill for years; she was protected against pregnancy, but she didn't know his sexual history... As if reading her mind, he pulled away and grabbed his pants from the floor. She turned to watch him find his wallet, retrieve a condom and quickly sheath himself.

"Come to the bed," she breathed, walking backwards, letting her hips sway a little as she moved, enjoying the way his eyes darkened to navy as he followed. She scooted up to the headboard and spread her legs.

He joined her, curled his large hands around her thighs, and tugged.

"Oh!" Her butt slid over the slippery silk sheets, unbalancing her. He palmed her sex positioning himself between her outspread thighs.

"I've wanted to taste you all night." Daniel bent his head. The heat of his mouth on her made her cry out. She wasn't a screamer. But as his tongue lapped her, and his finger rubbed against her stiffened clit, she could barely contain the sounds she was making. His other hand maneuvered one leg over his shoulder, and she did the same with the other, rubbing the soles of her feet down the rippling muscles of his back, pressing her heat into his face, seeing his dark head moving against her, in her.

The sex was perfect. He was perfect. Jesus, he must have done this a lot to be so good at it...

"Daniel..." His name was a husky groan, a plea to stop before she totally... Sensations made speaking difficult. "I can't..."

In answer, he thrust two fingers into her, moved his mouth to her clit and flicked his tongue over it again and again. His fingers curled, finding the hidden spot inside. "Jesus, Daniel, oh—"

Her back arched. She ground against his mouth, against his fingers. Abandoned. Overcome by ecstasy, surrendering to the bliss he created.

She cupped her breasts, tweaking her stiffened nipples, feeling an invisible cord tighten from her nipples to her core, flooding her with sensation. Her body jerked, she couldn't hold back any more, couldn't...her head thrashed side to side on the pillow, and Kathryn screamed his name, again and again.

How did this man have the ability to make her come so hard—so fast? In the aftermath of her orgasm, her legs felt heavy and languid.

Daniel angled his shoulders, re-arranged her legs to free himself from their hold, and travelled up her body to her mouth.

Mouth to mouth. Chest to chest, hip to hip. Every inch of her body touching his warmed. She breathed in his scent—spicy, woodsy, and fiercely masculine.

"You taste of honey. Maybe I'll call you Honey when we're in public—to remind you of this moment." His deep dimples reappeared.

She shook her head side to side. "I don't do nicknames. Or any of those cute little names."

"You think I might use them with someone else?" His brow arched. "That I might be calling someone else Honey behind your back?"

"It's just too easy. The moment you call a woman darling, babe or something like that you don't need to even try to remember their name."

"Jesus, that's harsh."

"It's true though. I mean, how would you like it if I started calling you Stud, Handsome, or Babycakes?"

"Babycakes?" His tone was so incredulous she couldn't help but laugh.

The mood switched from light to intense the moment he stroked the side of her face and stared into her eyes with a solemn expression. "While we're together there's no-one else for either of us."

He kissed her—first gentle, like the stroke of a feather, then as her mouth opened to accept him like a lover. Her fingers tangled in his dark hair, pressing against his scalp, keeping him close. His hardness was at her thighs and she automatically opened them wider, heat spiraling as his cock nudged against her wetness.

His hands bracketed her face; his touch was tender, gentle, at odds with the forceful thrusts of his tongue in her mouth, the insistent push of his hardness into her sex.

"You're so tight." Daniel stilled, giving her body time to stretch—to adjust to his size.

The feel of him inside was so delicious, Kathryn groaned. She tilted her hips up, encouraging him to sink further, adoring the feeling of his cock filling her. With each thrust, his balls slapped against her perineum. With every movement, he rubbed against her tender clit, firing a flash of sensation deep inside. Just when she thought she couldn't hold back anymore, he gripped the wooden bars of the headboard, sucked hard on her nipple, then bit it gently and increased the pace, burying himself deep, and fast, again and again.

"Oh…" She couldn't form words—couldn't hold the sounds inside. She bit her bottom lip in a futile attempt to.

"Fucking scream…we're checking out tomorrow," Daniel growled. He pounded in to her, using his grip on the headboard to hold his muscled chest in position above her as his hips jackknifed.

Kathryn couldn't seem to breathe in enough air; her labored, rapid breaths matched his. She raked her nails down his back, beyond caring if she scored his flesh. Wrapped her legs around him, and moments before Daniel's big body went into spasm, buried her face in his neck to stifle the sound of her passion, and screamed her release.

Chapter Six

Kathryn crept out of Daniel's bed in the early hours. Left a note on the pillow, saying she'd meet him for breakfast in the dining room later, and slipped back into her own room. After the first time they'd had sex, she'd joined him in the shower where he'd soaped every inch of her body, then fucked her up against the cold tile, rivulets of warm water slicking between their joined bodies.

Twice more during the night, they'd found each other in the darkness—and each time the sex had been even more explosive than the last. When she'd wakened this morning, he was curled around her, his cock nestled against her butt, his large hand on her stomach, his face in her hair.

Waking up like that was so damned perfect, the need to escape, to put some distance between them, had been urgent and unavoidable. So she'd run.

She couldn't be casual with Daniel. His focus on her was so intense, she found herself drawn to him like a moth to a flame. Craving more, even when she should be sated. He was like a dangerous drug she'd become addicted to after the first taste.

Going away with him couldn't be a good idea…not

when he had that effect on her.

She put on the black silk dress. Checked her watch—eight a.m.—and phoned Max.

"Hey, how did yesterday's meeting go?" Max's voice was bright and breezy.

Kathryn screwed her eyes up tight. Her friend was going to think she was a complete tramp.

"Well...he wasn't what I expected."

"I've only spoken to him on the phone," Max said. "What's he like?"

"He's gorgeous." *And so much more.* Kathryn swallowed. "I...I slept with him."

"You what?" Max's voice was so loud Kathryn jerked the phone away from her ear. "I don't believe it. You were supposed to be talking about the sex party—"

"We did talk about it. He upped the fee to two mill, and took me to a sex club."

"Two million?" Max sounded stunned. "He offered you two million...and took you to a real live sex club?"

"Yeah. Lucien Knight's Gateway club."

"That place is supposed to be awesome," Max breathed. "Full of celebrities and billionaires."

"Yes." She'd recognized a lingerie-clad British actress at some stage, but it had barely registered—she'd been much more focused on the feel of Daniel's hand at her back, at the heat building in her stomach, the wetness in her sex. "The atmosphere in the club is incredible. I got carried away, and ended up back in his room at the hotel, having crazy monkey sex."

"So where are you now? Are you still in his room?"

"No. I'm in mine. Next door. I'm coming home this morning."

"Have you made a decision about the party? Did you say yes?"

"I said yes." She smoothed her palms over her jean-clad thighs.

"You like him," Max said. "I can tell you really like him."

She did, but there was no possibility of a relationship. A man like Daniel… "He lives on the other side of the world. He's self-assured, powerful and independent. There's no way he fits into my world, and I can't see myself in his."

"Because of Hazzard Hall."

"More than that. Yes, I'm tied to the house. I have a responsibility to keep it safe, and there's the whole question of the roof needing repair. But as well as that, I have a life here—a career that at some time I need to get back to. I'm not a malleable twenty-something—I have my own plans."

"Kathryn…" Max's tone brooked no argument. "Face it. You're lost. Your father's illness and death changed everything. You had to leave the hospital to look after him, and now you're tying yourself to an old house—taking on the responsibility for keeping it intact so your ancestors won't be disappointed in you. Which is totally crazy. They're long gone—you can't let the needs of the house dictate your future. It's not going to be there forever, you're the last Hazzard, when you die…"

"Oh, Jesus. Don't start talking about my death."

"Okay, alright. That was out of line. But you know what I mean. The sex was good, right?"

"Fucking amazing," Kathryn groaned. "Totally fucking amazing."

"Well then." Silence for a moment, then Max spoke again. "We should talk. There's a ton of things to do to get the house ready for the party. Call me when you're home and I'll come over."

*****

She wasn't there when he woke. Daniel stretched his arms above his head. His cock stirred beneath the cool cotton sheet as he breathed in the lingering scent of her, remembered the taste of her skin, the sound of her husky voice breaking over his name.

She'd left a note saying she'd join him downstairs for breakfast.

Fuck that. He picked up the phone and called room service.

Ten minutes later, he tapped on her door.

She opened it—to his disappointment, fully dressed.

"Good morning." He kissed her, pulling her close and molding her curves against him. "Ready for breakfast?"

"I'll just get my bag."

He shook his head, and backed her into the room. "No need. They're sending breakfast up. We can eat in bed."

Her eyes widened. Darkened in awareness. "We can't just climb back into bed. There are things to do…"

"I know." There were a thousand matters to attend to. He needed to track down Cain, let him know he'd be taking some time off, and making sure his brother kept his goddamned phone on. But right now, only one thing mattered. "The most important thing to do is you, right at this moment."

Her smile lit up her face. "Desperate, huh?"

Daniel ground his erection against her stomach. "Yeah." Desperate. Totally desperate to flick her erect nipples with his tongue, slide his fingers into her honeyed heat. Take her, again and again. Normally after fucking all night, he'd be satisfied, but not with Kathryn. He wanted her as if last night had never happened. The feeling wasn't pleasant. It hinted at obsession, at an unfamiliar lack of control.

A discreet knock at the door heralded the arrival of breakfast. Daniel jerked the door open. "Put the tray over there." He waved at the low coffee table, shoved a note into the hotel employee's hand, and waited for the guy to leave before turning back to Kathryn. "Strip."

She chewed on her bottom lip. "I don't think that's a good idea."

He walked up to her, pushed a strand of soft hair back with his fingers, then let his fingers meander down the curve of her cheek, down her neck to the jut of collarbone. "You don't?" His mouth followed the trail his fingers had blazed, sucking hard on her neck.

Her back arched and her head flung back, pushing her gorgeous tits against his chest in a way that made it obvious that she didn't mean the words she'd spoken. "Because your body thinks that getting naked is a very good idea." He undid the side ribbon that fastened the wrap dress. Frowned to find her nakedness hidden. "You can throw this away. You won't be wearing a bra for the next week in Brazil."

Her head snapped up. "Brazil?"

He leaned in, spoke with his mouth mere millimeters from her full lips. "We're flying out to Brazil this afternoon—it's all arranged. We'll be alone in paradise, honey. No-one but me to see your beautiful naked body lying on the beach, swimming in the sea. No-one but me to hear you scream in fucking ecstasy as we fuck all day and all night."

Her hands came up, pressed against his chest. "I can't go."

*****

The change in him was instant, as though she'd dowsed him in freezing water. Daniel's arms fell to his sides. He took a step away. "You've changed your mind?"

"I never said I'd go away with you." She hadn't said she wouldn't either, hadn't said much of anything apart from frenzied words of encouragement the night before.

"Have you changed your mind about your house too?" There was no trace of the warm, teasing man of the night before. No smile.

He was acting as though she'd broken a promise—which she damn well hadn't. Kathryn refastened the tie and crossed her arms. "Of course not. I said I agreed to that, but I never said I'd..."

He stalked to the tray and poured a cup of coffee.

"Last night—" She swallowed. "What happened in the club and afterwards was wonderful but it wasn't real. There are a thousand things to do to get the house ready, I can't delegate the arrangements to anyone else, I need to be there."

"Do you always screw and run?" His tone was unemotional, almost conversational. As though the hours they'd spent together meant nothing, hadn't been special in any way. "Don't get me wrong, I have no problem if that's the way you normally operate—let a guy make you come in public then fuck you for hours in his hotel room after. I just wish you'd made it clear last night that all you wanted was one night. I wouldn't have bothered making arrangements."

Kathryn's hands curled into fists. "There's no need to

be so bloody insulting." Her back straightened. His words made what they'd done seem dirty, cheap. "We were both present last night."

"Yes." He placed the cup down carefully. "I guess you earned that extra million."

Something inside snapped. In rapid steps she was at his side and her hand struck the side of his face with an audible slap.

He just sat there, his cheek red from her hand. His dark-emerald eyes glittered. "If that's your idea of foreplay, honey, I'm not into it," he growled.

She'd never hit someone before, never lost her temper and resorted to violence. She clamped down on the instinctive urge to apologize. "I want you to leave."

He stood and walked out.

Chapter Seven

She'd been home for hours, and she was still steaming. So angry, she'd called Max and made some weak excuse about having a headache, and put off their meeting until the following morning. Max hadn't been happy, so Kathryn promised to ring her later.

She was giving a tour of the house tomorrow afternoon to an American group of history enthusiasts—something that had been organized months ago, but there would be time to run through all the arrangements that needed to be made about the sex party with Max before that.

So she burned off her anger by cleaning out the fireplace in the drawing room under the watchful eye of Tobias Hazzard, the first owner of the house, whose portrait had hung above the fireplace since the house had been built.

Had carried the steel bucket of ashes outside, and dumped them in the woods.

Still angry, she'd rubbed beeswax polish into the furniture.

"He's a complete idiot," she told Tobias. Confiding in his portrait was a common occurrence. "You'd hate him."

She's started vacuuming, but her cleaning frenzy was interrupted by a phone call from the auction house that had failed to sell the painting. She assured them she'd pay the consignment charge on receipt of their invoice.

At least she would have the money to do that now.

At the memory of Daniel's jibe about earning that extra million, her blood heated, and she turned the vacuum on again, and sucked up little black nuggets of soot that had fallen from the chimney.

Who does he think he is, anyway? The fact she couldn't stop thinking about him was driving her insane. Maybe once upon a time, she would have acquiesced to a man's ideas and plans, even if it weren't convenient. Maybe she would have been so stunned by the attention, and good sex, that she'd have jumped at the idea of boarding a plane on impulse, and flying away for a week in paradise.

Probably not though. Even in med school, there had always been responsibility tugging at her, keeping her grounded. Work, home, family. The only time she'd managed to get away was on the occasional holiday, and then she'd called the shots. She sure didn't need some man telling her what to do, and when to do it.

She kept her life strictly segmented, and didn't let her flings into her life for a reason. At home, she was the responsible, sensible, Kathryn Hazzard. A respectable member of her local society. She didn't get drunk in public, didn't dance on tables, or indulge in public displays of affection.

She kept that for her vacations—where she was just Katie, an English doctor without a reputation to protect. There, she could do and be whoever she wanted to be. She got drunk if she wanted to, kissed passionately in restaurants, and didn't worry about being spotted by anyone she knew, or scandalizing anyone.

She even danced on tables.

And never the twain should meet had been her unspoken motto for years. She was one person, but she lived two lives. Unfortunately, she'd made an exception in Daniel—and now working with him would be awkward. Especially as she couldn't turn off the stir of attraction that churned inside at the mere thought of his smile.

Weirdly, the memory of his smile and the hungry look in his eyes turned her on more than the memory of his naked body and the things he could do with his hands, with his mouth…

Stop it!

She turned off the vacuum cleaner, unplugged it, and stabbed the cord retractor with her foot. Then she and shoved it into a nearby cupboard. He'd acted like a jerk, throwing a hissy fit and being insulting just because she hadn't jumped into line the minute he'd made plans. Yes, he was delicious, the sex had been groan-worthy, but the affair was over.

Her hand slid, as it always did, over the polished mahogany banister rail as she climbed the stairs to her bedroom.

An hour later, she'd peeled off her grubby clothes and changed into sweats, caught up with her emails, and surfed the net for a while, all in an attempt to distract herself from calling Max and ranting about Daniel.

Then the phone rang. She was pretty sure Max was on the other end of the line—because curiosity was a bitch, and Max had been seething in it when they'd talked that morning.

So she answered it with, "I know I said I'd call you, but…"

"I don't remember you saying that," Daniel's deep voice murmured. "But I'm glad to hear I'm on your to-do list."

Her heart jumped around as though it had been shot from a cannon onto a trampoline. "I thought you were someone else." She closed her hand, rubbing her fingers over her palm as if to erase the muscle memory of slapping his face.

"I'm ringing you to say I'm sorry," he said. "I reckon slapping me was justified."

For a moment, she was speechless.

"Are you still there?"

"I didn't expect you to say that."

"Well, I was wrong—I own that. We had such a good time, I don't want the last memory you have of me to be the way I acted—bringing up the two mill was a cheap shot." He paused. "And talking of the two million, I didn't get your bank details. Under the terms of the agreement, you will receive half of the money now, and half after the party, so I need to get that finalized before I leave the country."

He's still in England?

"I thought you had to fly…" She actually had no idea of his schedule. "I presumed you had left the country."

"No. Cain and his business partner Ben—are taking some time to make another of their fantasies become real. They set off a few days ago for Machu Picchu, with a couple of bodyguards and a local guide. I don't expect them back for a week. Which is why I thought we could…" He cleared his throat. "But let's not dwell on my crazy vacation idea."

Listening to his voice, sitting on the edge of her bed, was making her muscles lax, and her thoughts turn to sex. *Again.* "If you give me your email, I'll send you the details so you can arrange a bank transfer," she said in her most businesslike voice.

"I could do that," he said. "Or you could open the gate and give them to me in person."

He's outside. She couldn't see the gate from her window, but stood and walked over anyway. For a moment, she just stood there staring out at the view, with the phone clutched to her ear.

"Kathryn?"

She hung up. Strode across to the gate release button at the side of her bed, and, before she could analyze her actions, pressed it. In a trancelike state, she left the bedroom, and tracked down the stairs. Putting Daniel Hunt in her rearview mirror had been her aim as she travelled back here this morning—mere hours ago. She should have made some excuse, she could and should still make an excuse, but she couldn't kid herself; she didn't feel able to.

At the heavy, mahogany front door, she shot the brass bolt, and rotated the ancient key. Then she turned the brass knob and opened the door. The noise of a powerful engine cut through the silent evening air. A couple of minutes later, a sleek black Mercedes came into view, pulled up outside the house and stopped.

She couldn't move.

Daniel's intent gaze met hers through the flimsy barrier of the windshield, and a blaze of heat started a slow burn at the expression on his face. Serious, focused, sexy as hell.

She held her breath as he opened the door and started

to move across the gravel sweep to the doorway where she stood. He didn't speak. Didn't smile.

She hadn't bothered with a bra when she'd changed, had just pulled on a ratty old T-shirt, and now her nipples peaked against the soft white cotton, making her painfully aware of just how much she wanted him.

His lips parted a fraction as he came close, then closer still.

He stepped into the house, and closed the door behind him. He didn't speak, just snaked a hand around her waist, slid it low to cup her ass, and then, in a sensuous move that made her insides clench, dipped his entire body so they were eye to eye and devoured her mouth.

He licked, he claimed, he plundered.

She walked backwards into the house, with her hands in his long hair, and their tongues tangling. His hands slid under her T-shirt, and when he discovered the lack of bra, he pulled the T-shirt up and off and tossed it over the wooden rack that held the Hazzard collection of walking sticks.

Panting, she did the same, loving the feel of his hard chest beneath her questing fingers, the ridges of his abs, and the deep grooves that arrowed from his hipbones beneath the low riding waist of his jeans. *Jesus, he's man candy personified.*

He backed her up until the edge of the mahogany, George III table pressed against her thighs. Then he looked over her shoulder at the polished tabletop with a gleam in his eyes.

"Don't even think about it—that table will not hold my weight." She glanced around. Here, in the hall, with its austere furniture and cold flagstone floor, there were no appealing surfaces to fuck on.

She took his hand and walked to the staircase.

He shadowed her so close it was as if they were one person. His hands wrapped around her, cupping her breasts from behind.

He kissed the nape of her neck.

She stopped on the stairs and leaned back into him, feeling his heat against her back, his hardness against her bottom. She tossed her head to the side, swinging her hair away from the curve of her neck.

He took the bait, abrading the exposed skin with his teeth.

Her hips pushed back against his pelvis—making it upstairs was not an option.

Her shoulders twisted, one forward one back. Interpreting her intention, Daniel's hands slipped from her breasts to turn her into his arms. Chest to chest. She was a step higher, bringing their faces into alignment. His gaze held hers, and once again he claimed her mouth. She couldn't look away, didn't want to break this connection by closing her eyes. And when he knelt and tugged down the soft fabric of her sweatpants, the strength seemed to leave her legs, washed away by a desire so powerful she shivered.

His face nuzzled the front of her panties.

Then he looked up, and with a wicked grin, took her hand and pulled her down to him.

The stair carpet, held in place by long, slender brass rods that she'd walked up and down for decades, was slightly worn, and rough against her soft skin. She'd never felt it before. She hadn't seen her house from this angle since she'd been a child, sitting on the stairs.

The memory dissolved the moment Daniel stroked

both hands over her stomach then upwards, in a sure exploration that left her breathless. She reached for his waist. *He needs to be naked.* Freeing him was difficult from the angle she was at, so he diverted his attention for a moment and shed what remained of his clothes.

Then got rid of her panties too.

Her feet were flat on one stair, her knees lax and open. He knelt a couple of steps below her, the width of his torso keeping her legs open as he closed his mouth over one of her erect nipples and flicked it with his tongue. *Wet.* Wet where his mouth was, and wet where her sex pressed against his stomach. As his mouth worked its magic, his body undulated up and then down. The light dusting of hair that feathered from his belly button to his cock, tickled with every slide, drove the desperate desire to have his rock hard cock flexing within her.

Her back arched, and he slipped a hand behind her, stroking the curve of the top of her butt. Her thighs squeezed the sides of his torso.

His head tilted up and a slow smile curved the corners of his mouth.

I want him. He knows it.

The hard stairs pressed against her bare back and she shifted, trying to get more comfortable. Noticing, Daniel frowned. This was far from being the ideal place, but the thought of stopping what they were doing in order to go upstairs where a bed awaited was impossible to contemplate. Not when she wanted him so badly.

"I need a condom," he muttered.

"Have you had a health check? For the party?" she asked.

"Yes."

"I'm on the pill. We don't need one." She wanted to feel him inside her without latex. Without anything between them.

His green eyes gazed into hers. "These stairs are hurting your back."

"It's okay," she whispered.

He shook his head. "Let's try this." He placed both hands on either side of her on the staircase, and in a sinuous move, flipped their positions so he was beneath and she was straddling him. Then he repositioned himself so that his cock brushed against her clit.

"Shit." Sensation flooded her. She was so wet…she couldn't wait…

His pelvis moved from side to side, rubbing himself all over her clit, her cunt, her thighs, her ass. Breathing heavily, she claimed his mouth and sucked in his lower lip.

His chest was rising and falling as fast as hers now, urgency making it impossible to continue teasing her any longer. His cock pressed on her upper thigh, moved higher, and then was at her entrance.

At fucking last.

He didn't make her wait. Didn't play any more games. Just thrust into her and filled her completely. He held her hips and in moves that revealed his extreme fitness, flexed up and down in a rapid rhythm that left her holding the bannisters with one hand, bracing her hand on the wall with the other, and coming faster than she ever had.

*****

We're screwing on the stairs. The thought, the actuality, was so absurd Daniel couldn't hold back a laugh. She was resting against him, her chest rising and falling as fast as his in the aftermath of their passionate coupling, and at the sound of his laughter, her head rose and she stared into his eyes.

Her beautiful mouth, reddened from his kisses, curved into a smile, and then she was laughing too. "That was crazy."

"Crazy good."

She pressed a light kiss to his mouth. "Yes, crazy good." His heart flipped. He was still inside her, more sitting than lying. He wanted to relax, to hold her close, but lying down meant the damned stairs would be hard against his back.

"This location is damned uncomfortable," he whispered. "Let's move."

She looked down to the point where their bodies were joined. "Are you trying to get into my bed?"

He grinned. "I admit it. Your shower too." After their fight this morning, he'd spent a couple of hours glowering at the wall and drinking coffee, and then realized what a complete idiotic prick he'd been to let her refusal of his plans bring their fling to a premature end. Sergei had assured him the house in Paraty would always be available to him—they would have that week in the sun sometime or other, he was damned sure of it.

But in order for that to happen, he couldn't let her just walk away. So he'd packed up, checked out, and hired a car to drive down here in the hope that his apology would change her mind.

Luckily, the need that clawed inside seemed to hold her in its grip too.

She tried to move, with difficulty, because her knees were flat against the stairs, and she couldn't get any traction.

"Here, scoot forward." He straightened his spine, held her close against his body, and pushed up to standing.

"That's impressive," she said. "But you really don't want to try to climb the rest of this staircase with me impaled."

His cock twitched. As did her eyebrows in response.

"Help me get down."

He gripped her close and bent his knees a little until he slipped out of her and she unwrapped her legs and managed to put her feet on the floor. She bent and picked up their discarded clothing from the stairs, offering a tantalizing glimpse of her bare bottom.

Then she turned. "Come on."

*****

So much for detachment.

Where Daniel Hunt was concerned, she didn't seem to have any. From the moment he'd appeared outside her house, staring at her with unashamed lust burning in his eyes, she'd lost the ability to be logical. She just wanted.

And he delivered.

Once she'd taken him upstairs into her bed, he'd delivered again and again, until her body should have been satisfied—should have had enough. But like an addict, she only had to see him, to breathe in his scent, to want him again.

Eventually, the sun vanished from the sky, and darkness took its place.

"Let's go out to dinner." Daniel pushed back a lock of her hair and tucked it behind her ear. "I'm starving."

"I could cook something…"

"You could. But I'd like to take you out."

A quick, mental inventory of the contents of her fridge made that idea more attractive. "Okay." She shifted her head from his shoulder, and threw back the duvet.

"Did you check out of the hotel in London?"
"Yes."
"Have you checked in anywhere else locally?"
"No." Their gazes locked. There was still time to book in to the local hotel—they could organize it in the village on their way to dinner. Or she could ask him to stay here. The sensible thing to do would be to put him up in a room in the local hotel. That way, she'd be able to keep some distance between them. She'd never had a lover in the house before, and was so close to becoming addicted to Daniel, that was definitely the smart, sensible option.

Screw smart.

Screw sensible.

"So stay here." Her heart pounded.

He didn't question her, didn't ask if she was sure about her decision. He just smiled, climbed out of bed and pulled on his jeans. "I'll get my bag, and then, honey, I'm taking you out to dinner."

Chapter Eight

When Daniel woke the following morning, the sun was high in the sky. Kathryn curled up behind him, her arm around his waist. He could tell from her regular breathing and unmoving form that she still slept.

He looked up into the canopy of the four-poster bed, to the faded pink rosettes formed of fabric that dotted the corners. Their color was brighter in the folds—indicating age. Looking out at the rest of the room that he'd paid no attention to the previous day, he noticed the details. A fine portrait over the fireplace. An old chest, bound with brass strapping next to a mahogany boot jack.

There was nothing modern about this room except the bookcase full of paperbacks.

She stirred.

Daniel turned around and brushed back a strand of hair that had fallen across the side of her face. "Good morning. Or should I say, good afternoon."

Her eyes flickered open. "What time is it?"

He reached over and picked his watch off the bedside table. "One-thirty."

"One-thirty?" She sat up, panic in her eyes. "Christ,

one-thirty! I have a tour coming this afternoon, I have to get ready!" She bolted out of bed.

"What time are they coming?"

"They'll be here at three." She opened the door of the mahogany wardrobe and clattered hangers. "I have so much to do. I have to light the fires, open the shutters…"

"I can help with all that." He climbed out of bed and dressed quickly. "Just tell me what needs doing."

She stood holding a dark brown tweed suit in one hand, and a cream shirt in the other. "Could you make us coffee? There's a coffee machine in the kitchen—God, you don't know where the kitchen is, do you…"

"I'll find it. What then?"

"Fires next. I light one in the hall and in the drawing-room."

"I'll do it. I'll see you downstairs when you're ready." She didn't even seem to be aware of her nakedness, but he was having a hard time stringing two words together with the sight of her before him.

"There's a metal bin for the ashes in the room at the bottom of the staircase." She tossed the clothes on the bed. Then she pulled open a drawer and picked out a cream colored bra and a pair of panties.

"How long will they be here?" He tried to ignore his growing erection.

"About an hour and a half." She strapped on the bra.

"Don't bother with panties."

She stopped and stared at him. "What?"

"Don't bother putting on panties. I like the idea of you giving a tour without them." He walked over and placed a hand over her bottom. "And the moment the tour is over I'd be taking them off again anyway."

A trace of red appeared in her cheeks, but she picked up the shirt, leaving the panties on the bed.

Daniel loaded up the coffee machine and flicked it on, then started on the next job he'd been given. His house in France had fireplaces, so he was no stranger to fire-building. He cleaned out the ashes, stacked the wood, and lit first one fire, then another. By the time Kathryn came downstairs, both were burning away.

"Come have some coffee." She had dressed into the tweed suit, with the cream shirt underneath. Her hair was twisted into a topknot, and she'd applied discreet makeup. A pair of low-heeled shoes completed the picture.

She looked like a librarian.

A very sexy librarian.

He followed her into the kitchen. "Tell me about this group," he said.

She was wound tighter than cable on a winch. Gulping coffee and checking her watch every second. "They're a specialist group with an interest in grand tour items." She looked at him. "Listen, I'm sorry, but I have to go and open up the house. Why don't you help yourself to some breakfast or something?"

*****

She'd never had the two different sides of her lives intersect before. In her tour clothes, she looked the part of chatelaine of Hazzard, but underneath…underneath she was preoccupied by the thought of the man she'd left in the kitchen. And underneath, she was naked. At his insistence.

Going commando in such circumstances gave her an illicit thrill.

She set out the collection of bronzes on the dining room table. Checked her watch again. *Half an hour to go.*

"There's a bus turning onto the sweep." Daniel stuck his head around the dining room door.

Damn, they're early. She cast her gaze around—everything was ready. "Do you want to join us?" She hoped he didn't.

"I'll go upstairs." He grinned. "You don't give them a tour of your bedroom, do you?"

"Heaven forbid. No. I'll just show them the ground floor." She crossed the room to him. "I'll see you later."

"An hour and a half. After that, I'm coming to get you." That wicked smile again, then he kissed her and walked away.

She met the group at the front door. Most of them had visited Hazzard the previous year, and gave her a warm welcome. It was strange to be here without her father. In the past few years, she'd taken over giving the tour, but he'd always been present.

Doing it without him hurt.

"Tobias Hazzard had his portrait painted by Anton Raphael Mengs while he was in Rome on grand tour in the early 1770s." She glanced up at Tobias's painted eyes.

The experts made notes, talked among themselves, asking and answering questions. Normally, she'd be captivated, listening to the curators of some of the most notable museums in the world discuss items in her home, but not today. Today the absence of her father filled her with sadness.

"Shall we go and examine the bronzes?" She opened the door to the dining room, and led them in.

When the tour was over, she walked them all to the front door, and smiled as one by one they shook her hand. One old lady, a retired curator from the Victoria and Albert

Museum, stopped and gave her condolences for the loss of her father.

"He was a great man," she said. "He'd be proud of you for keeping Hazzard Hall going."

Kathryn thanked her, hoping the woman was right. That the end justified the means. As they walked to the waiting coach, she turned the key in the lock and shot the bolt. Then she stood at the front door, ready to wave through the glass.

"Have they gone?" Daniel's voice was behind her.

She glanced back. He was standing at the bottom of the stairs; she could barely make him out in the shadows.

"They're just getting into the coach now." She stared out. Some of them were on the coach, already waving. She waved back.

"Don't turn around." His voice was close. A touch on her ankle. "Just keep smiling. They can't see." His hand slipped up her leg, pushed up the hem of her sensible skirt, until it bunched at her waist. She felt a breeze over her bare bottom.

"Open your legs. And keep waving."

Kathryn bit back a hysterical laugh. She shifted her feet so they were wider apart, smiled and waved as the coach started to move. And almost lost it as the heat of Daniel's mouth covered her.

*****

Daniel stayed for the next day and night, during which they only ventured out of the bedroom for meals. He didn't show any interest in learning about the house, instead focusing all his energies on making her come as powerfully and often as possible.

And over breakfast their third morning together, as

though a switch had been flipped he was all business. He insisted she open a Swiss bank account. Contacted Max by telephone and set a date for the sex party.

Then he told her he had a meeting in London, after which he was returning to the States. Kissed her, and left.

Chapter Nine

Money talks.

Or in this case, shouts. A team of professionals descended a couple of days later with detailed plans of how to transform the house. When it had acted as a film location, the transformation had been only partial—areas to be seen on camera were altered but areas behind the camera had remained the same. Now, the illusion had to be complete. The furniture was moved out to be stored at a secure storage facility, and new furniture brought in. Max had confided that instead of using a prop company, the Hunts had insisted on buying furniture from an upscale auction house.

Bedrooms had been completely redecorated in schemes of red and gold. Opulent velvet drapes were at the windows, and four-poster beds hung with filmy drapes of white and gold.

Even though the look wasn't one she would have ever chosen for her house, the bedrooms looked good. Not tarty, as she'd expected, but rather old Venice decadent.

Two rooms escaped the makeover; neither Kathryn's bedroom or her father's room would be used during the event, so they'd been left alone.

A large spider's web, big enough to capture a human fly, had been erected in one of the rooms, and a large cross in another, as well as a complicated piece of furniture that looked like a normal chaise longue in one configuration, but that Max had assured her converted into a spanking bench.

After two weeks of concentrated effort, the house was almost ready. The specialist workmen had cleared out, and this morning, Max would be arriving to talk through the logistics of the evening.

Kathryn dressed in the room that had become her refuge from the changes taking place in her home. The first tranche—a million—had been wired into the account set up for her in Switzerland, and she'd made arrangements to finally have the roof repaired, the large, ornate gates of Hazzard Hall electrified and had the drive resurfaced. The outstanding taxes had been paid, and the balance of the payment would be lodged directly after the party, ensuring that the house had a solid future. She should be feeling elated, freed from monetary pressure that had crushed her since inheriting, but instead the reality of living here forever, never being able to leave pressed down on her, stifled her.

She was owned. By a pile of rubble. And the expectations of the generations that had come before her.

When she died, there would be no-one to inherit. Many of her friends had done the whole marriage and children thing and she didn't envy them any of it. For years, she'd felt bad that she wasn't the maternal sort, but now she'd come to terms with it. Children weren't in her future, and she didn't need them to be.

Vacations were an option, but at the end of it, she'd

have to return to Hazzard. A place undeniably beautiful, but still a cage. The urge to escape it, to fly free was overpowering.

With a sigh, Kathryn brushed her hair and stared out of the window across the verdant green fields glistening in morning dew. She couldn't stop thinking about Daniel. He'd been different when he left, more detached. Maybe because she'd fallen into his arms the moment he crossed the threshold of her house, maybe because she'd forgiven his alpha display in the hotel so easily. She didn't know what to think, frankly.

But still…The mere sight of the giant web in the gold bedroom and the St Andrews cross in the room next door made her wonder what it would be like to be naked and restrained, unable to move or escape the attentions of a very determined mate.

In her imagination, there was only one man she wanted to play that part.

The doorbell rang. *Max*. She tossed her brush on the bed, and went to open the door.

As usual, Max dangled a white box of pastries from her fingers. Her blonde hair was bouncy, her eyes bright, and she seemed to quiver with unspent energy.

"Morning!" She dashed in. "How's it going?"

"Going good." Kathryn walked through the house to the kitchen with her friend by her side. "You're perky this morning."

"I've been up since five," Max confessed breathlessly. "And I only went to bed at one. The only time to do stuff like paperwork, orders and keep up with emails is out of hours. I'm up to here," she stabbed the air somewhere above her head, "getting stuff ready. Daniel wants me to clear an area in the field for a helicopter landing. Is that okay with you?"

Before Kathryn had a chance to respond, she continued. "Because Daniel, Cain and Ben want to fly in rather than come by car. I'll have to roll out a carpet to the makeshift helipad."

"A red one, I suppose?"

Max nodded. "Of course."

"Yes, that's fine."

"Good." Max pulled her cell phone out of a holster at her waist, and gave the okay to yet another group of contractors who would make that happen.

"I must admit you're damned good at what you do. You're a whirlwind. I hope he's paying you enough."

"Fifty grand," Max said proudly. "And he's paying all the bills on top of that. It's a great gig for me. I'll be able to set up my company with this."

"Company?"

"Yes. I'm starting a business," Max said. "I've become friends with some very powerful and interesting people over the last couple of weeks. And had some offers that would make your hair stand on end." She grinned. "There are a lot of depraved billionaires out there, and whole service industries catering to their every need. One thing that has become apparent is that the main criteria for doing business is trustworthiness. By doing this job for Daniel I've been accepted into all sorts of inner circles. I've decided to start up a business fulfilling fantasies. I'm calling *it Fantasies Made Real*. I've already got my next job."

Curiosity bit. "Well?" Kathryn reached into the box for a cream-laced confection.

"I can't mention the client of course." Max tapped the

side of her nose.

"Of course."

"But suffice it to say he's a very rich, very famous individual who everyone thinks is as conventional as they come, but he has a very unusual side."

"Surely he can get what he wants at a club? Or within a group of like-minded individuals if he's shy about being recognized?"

Max shook her head. "He wants to be kidnapped."

Kathryn felt her eyes widen. "He…"

"Yup. He wants to be grabbed off the street by a gang wearing balaclavas. In broad daylight. He wants to be chloroformed, treated badly, hit, and trussed up like a turkey. And after that he wants to be tortured." Her eyebrows quirked. "By a plus-sized dominatrix. He wants pain, and a lot of it. I won't go into the details but let's just say that it ain't compliant with the Geneva Convention."

"Does he want sex to be part of this adventure?"

"No. He wants to be denied sex. To be punished should he get an erection or become aroused in any way. That's his fantasy, and it's my job to make it happen."

"How on earth do you go about making something like that real?"

Max brought her hand up, rubbed her thumb against her middle finger. "Money. I have to choose people I can trust to abduct him. When this job is over, I'll be interviewing plus-sized dominatrices—there are a surprising number of them, by the way. And I'll need to rent an old warehouse to do the torture." She wiped a hand over her brow in a jokey gesture that made Kathryn smile. "I'll tell you, making fantasies real is a hard job."

"I sorta thought fantasies might be tamer than that."

"Fantasies can be everything. Can be anything. That's why they are so powerful. I want people to be able to come to me and spill their most intimate secrets, confess the things that they dare not voice with anyone else. And no matter how bizarre, I'm going to make it happen for them. Except murder. I'm staying away from death."

Kathryn felt floaty, disconnected from her body. Her best friend was sitting in her kitchen, calmly assuring her that she wouldn't be allowing murder in her new business, as though this was everyday stuff. They'd known each other for years—she never would have suspected that Max was open enough to embrace anything that anyone could throw at her. Her world tilted, as if she'd slipped through a portal into an alternate reality.

"Are you okay?" Max touched her arm. Her forehead pleated. "You're not shocked, are you?"

"I guess I am a bit." Kathryn swallowed. "It sounds as though this business could be dangerous—I mean if anything goes wrong, you're right in the middle, and you're not experienced in…" She looked carefully at Max. "I mean, I didn't think you were experienced in this sort of thing."

"I don't think anyone is experienced in kidnapping and organizing torture sessions. And you're right, I haven't much experience of the wilder side of life, but it appeals to me." She tilted her chin up a fraction. "You and I are so vanilla we might as well be shoved in a freezer with a paper wrapping labeled ice-cream on it. But after your experience in the Gateway Club I decided to try it out with a friend."

"Who?"

"Joel."

Max had often talked about her hot friend Joel.

They'd started out as friends, but lately had shifted the friendship to fuck-buddy status.

"He's been interested in the scene for a while, and under his guidance I felt able to live out some of my fantasies. I like multiple partners and exhibitionism, and he's into some stuff that's new to me, but pretty interesting, so…" Max licked cream from her fingertips and deftly changed track. "So…only five days to go. You haven't got your outfit yet, have you?"

Kathryn shook her head.

"That's what I thought. I have a selection in my car. I thought after cake we could go play dress up."

"I thought…" Her mind flickered back over the movie. There, the women had been clothed in floor length black cloaks and masked. When the time came for them to disrobe, they were wearing only tiny black thongs.

"Panties and stilettos?" Max scoffed. "Yeah, well. I have a clutch of courtesans arranged who will be playing those parts—all up for anything with the most beautiful, perfect bodies. But the guests are a different matter. They don't want to be told what to wear or how to act. Everyone will be issued a cloak at the door and they've been asked to keep it on while we reenact the opening scene from the film in the drawing-room, but once that is done we're allowing more freedom of dress for male and female alike. Not all the guys are interested in stalking around in tuxedos and not every woman wants to be practically nude." She rubbed her hands together. "So rubber, PVC, leather—what's your fantasy?"

*****

"It's questionable as to whether this woman is even pregnant," Daniel said.

"She could be. We had sex eight months ago, before I sold Bigtalk," Cain confessed. "We had a chance encounter in a bar, and now she says she's carrying my baby." He ran a hand through his hair. "I'll provide for her and the baby, of course, but I don't want to marry her. I barely know the woman."

Daniel opened the file on Emma Fitzgerald. The file he'd asked a discreet, private investigator to compile in the week since he'd learned of the woman's claim. "Around that time she slept with five other men. One of whom she appeared to be living with." He shoved the file across the coffee table to his brother. "I suspect the sale of Bigtalk and the potential to make a great deal of money is her main motivation in claiming you as her baby's father."

"If I've fathered a child, I'm going to support it." Cain's jaw tightened. "No kid of mine will grow up without a caring father."

Daniel would have expected nothing less from his brother. "The dates match your fling with her, though. You are to have no further contact with her, or anyone representing her. I have contacted a lawyer, who will negotiate a settlement if and when the child is born and only if a paternity test confirms you as the father. No contact. Understand?"

Cain shook his head. "No. I will pay her medical expenses."

Daniel frowned. "She could be a woman on the make, hoping to con you. You shouldn't give her anything without proof of paternity. There are tests she could have now that would establish paternity—first she should take those tests."

"I don't care if it isn't my baby. I'm paying her medical

expenses." Cain's jaw was tight. "If she needs someone to pay, I have the money, and paying the hospital bills doesn't mean I accept responsibility. Let the lawyer work something along those lines into the payment schedule. Tests on the baby in vitro could be hazardous—I won't agree to them. If the baby turns out not to be mine, at least it will have a good start in life."

"You're a pushover, do you know that?" Pride swelled at the sort of man his brother was—the sort of man who would look after a woman and put the wellbeing of her and her baby before financial consideration. Sure, it made him an easy mark, but paying the hospital bills was the right thing to do when even a possibility existed that the baby was his. "At least let me make sure that the payments are made directly to the medical professionals involved—not just given to her. I don't want you taken advantage of."

Cain nodded.

"Tonight you and Ben get to live your fantasy. One that I, and a very expensive team, have worked hard to put together. All potential pregnancy threats have been taken care of, and all you have to do is enjoy yourself. Drink. Indulge. Everyone at the party is a sexual adventurer, nothing is off limits. All you have to do is live out your fantasies. Every single twisted one. Can you do that?"

At the thought of tonight, of seeing Kathryn again, Daniel paced around the London hotel suite like a caged lion. He wanted to brush off his brother's problems. Wanted to go back to her.

"What is it with you?" Cain asked, in much the same manner as he had for the past two weeks. "Are you ever going to open up and talk to me?"

"I'm fine." What had gone on between him and

Kathryn Hazzard was no-one's business. But tonight, he'd see her again. Two nights and days in her bed had changed him. After their lovemaking, he'd slept like a baby, and had reached for her the moment his eyes opened every morning.

What was between them was more than sex. And the knowledge that he was beginning to feel far more than he wanted to—the fact he was becoming attached—had sent alarm spiraling through him.

Putting some distance between them seemed sensible, so he'd made his excuses, and retreated. He'd taken a beautiful model to dinner, had even gone so far as to try to take her to bed after, but the memory of Kathryn slipped between them like a Perspex shadow, making even touching his companion impossible.

She was in his system. Coursing through his veins like a deadly drug. Poisoning him for every other woman. It couldn't continue.

Cain was still waiting, looking at him with that searching expression that was damned near impossible to ignore. "You're worse since we landed in London," Cain said.

"Worse?"

"Grouchier. More restless. You're stalking around like a lion in need of tranquillizing."

"When I was here last, I met someone." The words were ripped from him. "We'll be seeing her again. Tonight."

Cain's eyes widened. "She's a member of the Gateway Club?"

Daniel shook his head. "She's our hostess. The woman who's got me so wound up owns Hazzard Hall." The thought of seeing her again, smoothing a hand over her soft skin, splaying a hand over her stomach and pulling her close against his body made his cock stir.

"The woman who owns Hazzard Hall, Kathryn Hazzard is…" Cain spluttered.

"Bewitching."

Chapter Ten

Kathryn stood at the top of the staircase, her features partially hidden by an ornate, jet-black, feather mask that covered her from cheekbones to hairline. Her palms were damp. Nerves tightened in her stomach and a bead of sweat trickled the length of her spine.

Sounds from downstairs drifted to where she stood. The keyboard player had arrived an hour ago, and for the past half hour a never-ending stream of expensive vehicles had delivered the guests. Max was busy at the front door, welcoming everyone, giving them masks and cloaks, and ushering them into the downstairs rooms.

She pulled in a shaky breath, breathing in the potent scent she'd applied to her pulse points earlier. Smoothed a hand down the floor length cloak and straightened her spine.

This was her house, but tonight she was just an anonymous guest, like everyone else. She'd checked the guest list to ensure no-one she knew in real life was attending. Every guest had been screened, and signed confidentiality agreements—they'd been driven to the event by a crew of professional drivers, all of whom Max vouched for unreservedly.

There was no possibility of exposure.

Except of the personal kind...She swallowed. She had one task tonight. To make sure everything went off as planned. Tonight was business, not pleasure. When the helicopter arrived, she'd be professional. She wouldn't disgrace herself by reacting should Daniel take full advantage of all the sexual temptations on offer—should screw someone else. What had been between them was a one-time thing. He'd shown little reaction when he left a couple of weeks ago, couldn't have made it more clear that their relationship was a sexual one, rather than something more.

Somewhere along the line, she'd lost her objectivity. Had started to feel she wanted more. The time had come to protect her heart. *I'm over it. I'm over him.*

"There you are!" Max appeared at the bottom of the stairs and started toward Kathryn. "What are you doing up here? The party's downstairs."

With every step the cloak parted to reveal a glimpse of Max's spectacular legs.

"I'm gathering my courage," she admitted. "How's it all going?"

"Great!" Max's scarlet painted mouth curved into a wide smile. Her mask matched Kathryn's but was made of feathers in shades of white and pale-pink instead of black. The Swarovski crystals inset around the eyes glittered. "The helicopter should be here in a few minutes. Come on." She linked her arm through Kathryn's and together they descended the staircase.

Kathryn started to relax as she entered the hall. The two butlers she'd met earlier were busy greeting new arrivals and long-legged hostesses were accompanying them into the drawing room. Masses of exotic, hot-pink orchids sprang from a glossy black pot on top of the fireplace and on the mahogany table between the two doors that led from the hall into the drawing room and dining room. A fire blazed in the hall fireplace, and as in the movie, the lighting was subdued and intimate.

Max's cell-phone buzzed with a message.

"They're here."

"Should we go out and greet them?" The etiquette of the evening was difficult to gauge—Cain and Ben were living a fantasy that had already been diluted by arriving by helicopter instead of by car.

"No. Let's watch from inside."

Kathryn followed her into the drawing room. Normally in the evenings full-length wooden shutters would cover the tall sash windows, but tonight they'd been left open to show the darkened landscape, painted by the silvery glow from the full moon. A searchlight painted the helipad from a large black helicopter floating above like an oversized dragonfly. The guests clustered by the windows like exotic animals in their black cloaks and ornate masks, watching the spectacle unfold. Yesterday, workers had removed part of the wooden fence that separated the field from the house and laid a red carpet across the grass to the landing spot.

Kathryn's heart was pounding fit to burst as the craft lowered to the ground and three figures made their way up the red carpet to them.

All three wore tuxedos and were masked, but Daniel was unmistakable. He was taller than the others, leaner, and the way he walked made desire curl inside. His midnight black hair whipped in the wind blown up by the circling blades, and where the others were clean-shaven, he was still sporting a beard.

As the entourage passed the window and continued around the house to the front door, Max turned. "Which one is Daniel?"

"The tall one."

"The one who looks like a pirate?"

"Yeah." Kathryn's insides clenched at the thought that right about now, they'd be walking through the front door. "I guess we should go meet them."

Max shook her head. "Daniel doesn't want anything to threaten the fantasy for Cain and Ben—I can approach him, but only discreetly, when they've entered the room."

Heat diffused through her, making her palms damp. Despite her misgivings, her entire body tingled at the thought of seeing Daniel again. She swiped her tongue over her lips and swallowed. The cream silk bodysuit she'd chosen for this evening was pure vanilla compared to some of the outfits worn by the other partygoers under the cloaks they'd donned for this portion of the evening—but she didn't feel body confident enough to wear anything more avant-garde. She looked good. More than good. And there was only one man she wanted to peel the cloak off her.

Even if she was supposed to be denying herself.

The music changed, and the mood in the room shifted. Long, sonorous tones, dramatic and haunting, filled the room as Daniel, Cain and Ben entered. Just as in the movie, guests put down their drinks, rearranged their cloaks and fell silent.

Like a ringmaster in a dark circus of delights, Max walked in a circle around the center of the room. Dark clad figures silently moved into place, forming a circle. A shiver ran up Kathryn's spine as Daniel gazed around the room.

He was looking for someone. Looking for her.

The coterie of long-legged women hired for the evening stalked one by one into the center of the circle, and as the music played, shed their cloaks like beautiful butterflies shedding their cocoons. Clad only in tiny black thongs, their bodies were total perfection. The air seemed to vibrate with unspoken desire as the first of the women walked to Cain, took him by the hand and walked him away into the next room.

One by one, five women chose a man, as had been arranged in Max's run through the night before.

As the last woman set her sights on her target— Daniel—something bitter and dark rose in Kathryn. There were no surprises thus far, as a VIP he was one of the men to be looked after, but knowing it was completely different to living it.

Living it was hell.

His mouth curved in a smile that stole her breath as the near-naked woman stopped before him. Her hand rested on his dark cloak, just above his chest. *Now, he'll lose the cloak…*

Daniel undid the clasp at his neck, and the cloak fell to the ground.

And now, he'll take her hand, walk away with her and…

Daniel murmured something to the woman, took her hand, and passed her on to another.

His gaze swept the room until he found her. Eyes locked on hers, he started walking. Anticipation clutched her heart, stole her breath, as he tracked across the Aubesson as though nothing in the room could interest him, could deflect him for an instant from his goal. Her mouth was dry, and she swallowed and forced back the instinctive urge to flee. In scant moments, he was there—right in front of her. Her heart pounded a frantic drum solo.

"Hi."

With just that one word, the time apart seemed to dissolve, forcing her back to the time they'd spent together.

"Hi." She wanted him with an overwhelming fierceness.

"Hello, Mr. Hunt. I'm Max." The voice from next to her shook her back to reality. "Glad to meet you."

Daniel's focus shifted to Max. "It all looks great, Max." He flashed her a smile. "If you'll excuse us?" Not giving Max a chance to reply, he snaked an arm around Kathryn's waist. "We have some catching up to do."

Then he was moving, pulling her along with him out of the room full of people back into the entrance hall, as though he knew the downstairs layout of the house, had some idea where he was going. Ignoring everyone and everything, he twisted the handle of the door into the library, and entered the dimly lit room. The revelers hadn't started to move around the house yet, so the room was empty. A fire made of heavy logs cut from the estate blazed in the fireplace, illuminating the room with a flickering glow. Daniel turned the ancient key in the lock. Took her hand, and brought her before the fire.

One hand slid behind her hair to cup her nape, and the other released the jeweled clasp at her throat that held the cloak in place. In a whisper of fabric, the heavy cloak fell to pool at her feet, leaving her revealed in the wisp of silk and satin.

Their masks were next. He took them both off, and dropped them to the floor.

His gaze travelled slowly over her breasts. They felt full and heavy under his lazy perusal, and her nipples tightened to hard nubs under their light, silk covering. She wanted him to suck each aching peak into his mouth, push the fabric aside and lave them with his tongue. The thought of his beard brushing the sensitive skin on the side of her breasts as his mouth sucked made dampness flood her. With just a look, this man turned her to boneless, made her want.

She made a tiny noise, and his eyes darkened. He placed a hand on her neck, trailed long fingers straight down between her aching breasts, the soft fabric covering her stomach, to his destination, the juncture of her thighs.

"I like this." His deep voice was almost a growl as he stroked the intricate lace at the garment's edge.

"It opens. Underneath."

He arched a dark eyebrow, making him look every inch the pirate he was. "You came prepared?"

She'd thought of nothing else but having him inside her for weeks. Clenching her inner muscles around his hard cock, and feeling him thrust inside her. Yet admitting it… "It is a sex party, after all. Everyone came prepared this evening."

He scowled. "Don't pretend you planned for a moment to play with anyone but me." He trailed his lips down her neck, flicked his tongue over her collarbone. "You planned this for me. Don't lie."

Telling the truth, without him admitting it too made her vulnerable. "And you?"

Long, skilled fingers found the tiny fasteners under her sex and flicked them open. His slid his palm between her legs, and pressed up firmly. The sensation was so intense she let her head fall back, closed her eyes and groaned.

"I haven't been able to stop thinking about you, about this, since I walked away," he admitted. "I've lain awake night after fucking night with the biggest hard-on I've ever suffered, thinking of tasting you, of fucking you. I haven't been able to screw any other woman—you're in my head. My entire body craves you, and tonight—tonight we get to have each other. Over and over, until neither of us can see straight."

We get to have each other.

"Fuck me, Daniel."

The words, muttered huskily, had an immediate effect. Daniel moved his hands to the globes of her bottom, and plundered her mouth. His tongue thrust into her mouth urgently, tasting her over and over as breath stalled in her lungs. Her hands were everywhere, spiking through the stands of his hair, massaging his scalp, pulling him closer—if that were even possible. He walked forward, she stepped back until the heat of the fire warmed her naked bottom.

"Turn." He twisted her around, pushed down the straps of the bodysuit to expose her breasts, and cupped them in his hands.

Heart thundering, Kathryn reached out for the mantel of the fireplace, gripping onto the cold marble with shaking hands. His fingers tugged at her erect nipples, teasing, tormenting. Half aware of the picture she must make half-naked in his arms, the heat of the fire warming her skin, she braced her legs apart, and pushed her bottom back into his groin.

She could feel him, hard, big and ready.

"Fuck." One hand stroked down her body and slipped between her legs. His finger dipped inwards, rubbing her clit.

Kathryn arched her back and felt the fire's heat in front of her, warming her breasts. She gripped harder onto the mantelpiece, dimly aware of the precariousness of her position as his fingers moved into her wet heat. Then looked up into the face of her great aunt captured in the framed photograph dead center.

What would her aunt have thought had she actually observed such a sight? Had anyone, ever, been naked and desperate in front of this fire?

His guttural groan flared across her nerve endings, causing a burst of heat to suffuse her body.

"Daniel." In one quick move, she jerked upwards, straightening and leaning back onto him. She wanted more, needed more. Needed him closer. Inside. She sure didn't need to be looking at her relatives when that happened.

She turned in his arms, and before she could register it, he'd moved with her in his arms and backed her up to the floor to ceiling bookcases that covered the wall. On the opposite wall, portraits of her ancestors gazed down, or stood to rigid attention, perfectly posed in landscapes with dogs and horses.

It's my house. My life.

And she would live it. Would own it—all of it. The house, her life, the choices she made. Daniel's mouth covered hers. Her fingers unfastened his bow tie, then worked to unfasten the buttons of his swan white shirt. She tugged it from the waist of his trousers, pushed it from his sculpted chest, then ran her hands over every inch of his hard warmth. With every breath, she breathed in the scent of him, warm, male, spicy. Her fingers worked at the button of his tuxedo pants, fumbling in the urgent need to free him.

He must be feeling the desperation to be naked too, for he edged away for a moment to help her, then shoved his pants and boxers down, springing free.

"I can't take it slow, I need you too much." His fingers moved in and out of her opening. Firm fingers moved over her tenderest place with a mastery that made her gasp. She didn't need more foreplay, couldn't bear not to have him inside her. Her hand curled around his erect cock, moved up and down in a sinuous motion that earned a hissed intake of breath.

Hearing the proof of the effect she had on him made her happy. Beyond happy—ecstatic. Her other hand reached around him, to caress his firm buttocks, which flexed in response to her touch.

In one smooth move, he hiked her up so her back was against the cold glass that covered the family bibles, the tomes of leather bound volumes embossed with the family coat of arms collected by Hazzards long dead.

She wrapped her legs around his waist.

His cock teased her slick entrance. He held himself with one hand and rubbed the tip over her swollen nub. Licked her lips with a carnality that left her struggling to breathe. Then slipped his cock and his tongue into her at exactly the same moment.

God, the feel of him stretching me, filling me so completely...

Beyond glorious. She gripped his naked shoulders, dug her fingers in to his smooth flesh, and held on as he increased the rhythm of his thrusts, somehow shifted the angle so he pressed against her G spot with every movement. Need became audible in the gasps, the groans, the frantic noises she couldn't help but make as Daniel's hips flexed and pistoned, pounding into her. His mouth moved to her neck, and the sensitive skin stung as he nipped it with his teeth then fastened his mouth over the bite and sucked gently.

If only she could move, could touch more of him… the thought evaporated in an instant as the arm holding her in place tightened. Demonstrating immense control, he built the speed to frantic. With each thrust, her sensitive clitoris rubbed the base of his cock, firing sparks of sensation until she couldn't hold back anymore—couldn't—the pressure, the heat building in her core was impossible to resist, impossible to hold back.

"Come for me," Daniel groaned against her neck.

"Kiss me," she managed to murmur. The moment his head rose, she claimed his mouth, thrusting her tongue inside in a crude echo of what he was doing to her body. Her arms wrapped around his shoulders, fingers spiked into his hair, rubbed against his scalp as her orgasm hit.

He continued thrusting as her inner walls contracted around him, holding him in her tight grip.

"Fuck. Kathryn!" With one final thrust Daniel came, his whole body rigid as his cock buried itself deep and his seed spilled into her.

Chapter Eleven

His heart pounded fit to burst. Breathing—actually getting enough air into his lungs, was difficult. She clenched around him like a silken vise, and without the condom, he could feel every single curve and dip inside her.

His leg muscles burned, and his tense biceps ached with the effort of holding her in this impossible position. "I have to put you down." Damn, his body was close to collapse as he helped her slide her feet to the ground then, with reluctance, eased out of her.

Wordlessly, she grasped his hand, and moved to the huge, leather chesterfield sofa. She still wore a scrap of fabric, the top pushed down to reveal her magnificent breasts, and the bottom buttons open. Now, she fiddled with a complicated arrangement of straps at the side, and unfastened them, throwing the garment to the ground. She lay down and scooted back, leaving plenty of space for him to lie beside her.

Snuggling wasn't his thing. Never had been. Until her.

Her skin was so white—so soft. He fitted his body against hers—face to face—chest to gorgeous tits. Couldn't hold back a sigh as she arched her back and pressed herself against him—slid one leg between both of his in a tangle so completely natural, all his muscles relaxed into the warm afterglow.

"I'm supposed to be monitoring this party," Kathryn whispered, "instead of curling up here with you."

"And I'm supposed to be making sure my employers are having a good time." He smoothed a hand over the curve of her hip. "It looks as though both of us are neglecting our duties."

"I guess we should move. Check out what is happening in some of the other rooms."

"Worried?" She sure didn't look it. She looked satisfied, and languid. The fact he'd made her so spread a warm feeling of satisfaction through his chest. "Bored with me already?"

Her face flushed. "I don't think I'd ever be bored with you." The ring of honesty in her tone should have set off alarms, but strangely, didn't. He felt the same way. When tonight was over he'd be sending Cain and Ben back to the States full of tales of their erotic adventures and insisting on that holiday. The clear green waters of Paraty, soft white sand, and the seclusion of Sergei's island paradise hadn't been cancelled, only postponed.

"I should go and check with Max that there are no problems." She frowned and her mouth turned down at the corners. "I'm hungry. Are you hungry? There is an amazing selection of food set up in the dining room. And you haven't even seen the changes we've made to the house—"

"I've seen enough." In truth, all he'd wanted to see was her, naked. His gaze shifted to the portraits on the walls. "Are these all your ancestors?"

"Yup," she said. "They are all Hazzards. Most of them

actually lived in this house too. I'm glad we moved from the fireplace, I looked up to see Great-aunt Agatha"—she glanced over to the mantelpiece—"staring straight into my eyes. It almost put me off my stride." Her mouth curved into a smile. "I've never had sex with anyone in the house before. Except you."

Her words made no sense. This was her house, her home. How could she never…

"I lived in an apartment for a while, before my father became ill," she explained.

"And that's where you had sex." The words tasted foul in his mouth. He didn't want anyone else touching her— the very thought that others had, made irrational anger bubble up inside. "Were there many before me?" Being jealous, caring, was ridiculous.

Her body stiffened. "What?" she leaned back from him, untangled her legs from his. "What the hell sort of question is that? I don't have to tell you about my previous lovers. I've been celibate since you, and I certainly don't intend to draw you a picture or write you a list."

"Have others been inside you the way I have?"

Her eyes widened. "What is this— Are you," she frowned. "Are you jealous?"

"Yes. Kathryn. I am." Owning the emotion felt good. Felt honest. He traced a finger down her straight nose. "I can't bear the thought of anyone else fucking you. Of having fucked you. I want you all to myself." He shrugged. "That may seem primitive, but that's what you've reduced me to. You can ask me the same questions."

Her eyebrows rose. "I really don't want to know the answers." She chewed on her bottom lip. "I'm thirty-five, Daniel. I've been a woman for a while. During that time

I've had many lovers. None of whom I've slept with in this house, but yes, I have screwed people in my apartment, and I have been on holiday alone—met men, and slept with them. Not because I'm a slut, but because I have needs and desires. I've never had a one-night stand, but I've had brief, mutually satisfying encounters with temporary partners." Her eyes blazed into his. "Haven't you?"

"Of course." Obsessing over her previous partners was beneath him—futile. Didn't make one shred of difference to the here and the now. "I guess we should go out and enjoy this party."

"I'm sort of enjoying this party already." She grinned. "But yes, you're right. Pass me my clothes?"

The wispy fragment could hardly be described as clothing, but he sat up and picked it off the floor and handed it over—turning his back to her as he dressed.

*****

Leaving the library was like diving out of a lifeboat into the ocean. A carnal sea of people having fun, down and dirty fun. Drinking, touching, talking, fucking. The movie had been dramatic and weighed with dark overtones, but none of those were present tonight. Instead, the mood was heady, light, and, despite all her concerns earlier, joyous.

The ancestors staring down from the walls might even smile at the proceedings, if they could. The night was a celebration of all the good things in life. People openly celebrating their humanity.

"I want to go upstairs," Kathryn said. "And see if I can find Max."

"Okay." Daniel kissed her quickly. "I don't see Cain anywhere, and I sure don't want to catch him in the act so I'll stay down here and get something to eat." The feast in the dining-room had been plundered, but there were still laden platters of food available. "I'll be here." He tugged on the sides of her floor-length cloak, ensuring it covered her totally, like a parent covering up a teenager before letting them out to a disco. His eyes were dark with vestiges of passion spent, his touch proprietorial.

He was a man who liked to be in charge. Liked to own. The sort of guy she normally avoided like the plague, because she was no nervous virgin, looking for an alpha. They'd moved past being stereotypes to each other. He wasn't a cardboard cutout, and neither was she. *I like it.* The truth was undeniable, they'd moved past the pretense of limits to what he could or couldn't say to her, what she would or wouldn't say to him. She wanted him in exactly the same way as he wanted her. "While I'm away—look, don't touch," she whispered.

His wide grin transformed his face. "Want me all to yourself?"

"Damn right."

He ground his mouth onto hers, stole her mouth with a kiss that made desire flood her again, almost made her give up the plan to check on Max and do something considerably more interesting instead.

She pulled back. "Enough. I have to go." She picked up their masks and put hers on.

"Hurry back."

The heavy cloak swung around her ankles as she stepped onto the curving staircase. Lamps from downstairs cast shadows on the painted walls. The crystal chandelier from the top floor sparkled. The large window on the landing, filled in with colored panes of glass that formed the Hazzard coat of arms, was dark as she climbed higher.

The sound of music was barely audible here, she had to strain to hear it—most of the guests must still be downstairs.

A shiver of awareness flickered down the length of her spine.

She whipped her head around, down the staircase, then up, to the stairs continuing to the next floor. From her position, the view was occluded. Was someone lurking in the shadows? "Hello?" Her words weren't met with an answer. She took a step up onto the next flight, breath catching in her throat—*no-one*. Kathryn took in a deep breath, then blew it out slowly. *My imagination's playing tricks on me.* But still a sense of disquiet lingered. A feeling of being watched.

Straightening her spine, she stepped down the corridor to the bedrooms. She stopped outside the first room. The door was closed, but there were evidently people inside, muffled sounds came from within. As in the Gateway Club, the rule was that if a door was closed you didn't enter—if people wanted to invite others in, or wanted to be watched the door would be left open or ajar. A glance down the corridor revealed two open doors.

She started down there, then paused. The sense of foreboding, the feeling that something was horribly wrong, was so strong she turned and looked back the way she had come.

She started at a sound—a shuffling of feet on the carpeted stairs, then a figure rounded the corner. *Max.*

Something was terribly wrong. The black cloak and mask Max had been wearing were gone, and her friend was clad only in black satin and leather lingerie. Her makeup was mussed, and black trails of mascara ran down her cheeks. When she spotted Kathryn she cried out and walked forward on shaking legs.

Kathryn ran to her immediately. "What is it? Are you okay?" She checked Max for injury. "Did someone hurt you?"

Max was sobbing, trying to say something, but incoherent. "Upstairs..." She waved an arm behind her. "Help...go help her..."

"You need to sit down." Kathryn helped Max to the chair at the top of the stairs. "Someone is injured?"

Max nodded. "Help her. I don't know if she's breathing."

"Stay here." Kathryn breathed in deep and took the stairs two at a time.

The top floor was quiet and still. There were no people up here, no sound. Kathryn shivered, even though the temperature was constant. She rounded the top of the stairs and, as if compelled by an invisible force, walked down the corridor to the room with the giant spider-web set up.

The door was open wide. Willing herself to keep going, not to turn back and seek Daniel, she walked in. A woman was cuffed onto the outspread strands, her black leather outfit open breast to crotch. Her body sagged from bound wrists, and long blonde hair covered her face. On the floor lay a discarded silver leather mask.

An unmoving body of a man, stripped to the waist, lay on the floor.

Oh my God! On shaking legs Kathryn ran to the woman. *I shouldn't touch anything—this may be a crime scene.* The thought that the woman might be dead stole the breath from Kathryn's lungs. She breathed in deep, again and again, trying to center herself, trying to stop herself falling completely to pieces at the scene before her. The woman's hair was over her face, so long, it hung lower, covering her left breast. Gently, Kathryn's eased it back. A long, black silk scarf was around her neck—not so tight as to cut off her breathing, but the reddened skin on her neck revealed that at some stage this evening it had been.

Kathryn undid it and dropped it to the ground. "Can you hear me?"

The man on the ground would pay for this.

A touch to her neck confirmed that the woman's skin was warm, and a press to her neck revealed a pulse—weak, but present. The leather cuffs on the spider-web were holding her entire weight; help would be needed to support her before undoing them.

Kathryn turned her attention to the man on the floor. He lay on his back, and his black leather mask glistened with a trace of blood from an oozing gash on his forehead. Further examination revealed a bump the size of a goose egg behind the cut, as though he had been struck. She searched the ground for a weapon, then noticed blood on the corner of a heavy table beside the bed. The rug covering the wooden floor was wrinkled and bunched.

It must have shifted on the polished boards.

She checked for, and found a pulse. He didn't stir as she eased the black leather mask up and off. Her fingers probed the gash on his head. The smell of alcohol hung strong around him. His unconscious state could have been from the injury, or from the amount of drink he'd consumed—it was impossible to tell.

Two things were sure. She needed an ambulance.

And the man was no stranger.

HAZZARD BLUE

Chapter Twelve

Daniel had checked out the rooms downstairs without finding his brother. Ben was lounging on one of the sofas in the drawing-room with three beautiful women. One crouched on the ground at his feet, the perfect globes of her ass on display in a tiny thong as she bent over him. From the look on Ben's face, his cock was in her mouth.

Another of the women had just stripped off her top and was kneeling on the sofa, edging her erect nipple to his mouth.

Maybe Ben knew where Cain was, but there was no way in hell Daniel would go over there and ask. Watching men he knew…well, he could think of a thousand things he'd rather do. More than a thousand. *A million.*

He turned and stalked back into the hall.

"Hi." A stunning redhead dressed in a red and silver basque and matching panties walked straight to him, her painted mouth curving into a smile. "I'm Angelique. Shall we get a drink?"

Ordinarily, he'd take her up on the offer. The woman was gorgeous, with curves most men would find impossible to resist. But now, he only wanted one woman. "Sorry, darlin', I'm waiting for someone."

She pouted. "Well, if she or he doesn't turn up…"

"She. But let me get you a drink anyway." He hailed a passing waiter, snagged two glasses of champagne from a silver tray and handed one over.

"A true gentleman." She tipped her glass to his. "Thank you."

"Daniel."

He turned at his name, to see Kathryn walk into the hall from the staircase.

"Have fun," he said to the redhead before turning away from her and walking to the only woman in the house who held his interest. She wasn't smiling. Her shoulders were stiff, and she was worrying her bottom lip with her teeth. He couldn't make out more of her expression because of the black-feathered mask that hid her features. "Are you okay?"

"*I* am. But we have a situation upstairs. I need your help," she said with quiet determination. "Immediately."

They climbed the stairs. At the top, Max sat slumped in a chair. She didn't look up as they approached, just stared at the floor as though drugged.

Kathryn stopped and placed a hand on her friend's shoulder. "Max," she said in a soft voice. "I know you're upset, but I need you to pull yourself together. I need you to get dressed, and help us."

Max's head rose. Her eyes were bloodshot, and tearstained.

"They're going to be okay, but we need you, Max. I need you to focus."

Slowly, Max nodded.

One of the security team hired for the evening

blocked the way to the second flight. "No-one has gone up," he said to Kathryn. "Four or five people came up and went into the bedrooms—" he waved an arm down the corridor—"but I explained the top floor is off limits, as you asked."

"Good. Keep everyone away."

Kathryn reached for Daniel's hand. "Come on."

"What the hell is going on?" The cloak and dagger routine was getting old. Kathryn pulled a key out of the pocket of her cloak and unlocked the room at the top of the stairs. He followed her inside. "I just have to get something." She opened the wardrobe and picked up a battered, brown leather bag. "There has been an assault." Her tone was dull, unemotional. "It's bad." Her voice wavered and her fingers tightened into fists. "There is a woman unconscious on the spider-web. I need you to support her while I unbuckle the straps."

Shock thundered through him. "A sex game gone wrong?"

She breathed in quickly. "She's injured. There are marks on her neck, and there was a scarf—I think she was asphyxiated."

"Christ." Anger flared. "Who?"

She ignored his question.

"Do you mean to say the guy involved didn't go for help?" Any man who would hurt a woman, and not get her aid was beneath contempt. "We need to shut this party down, find out who is responsible and…"

"There's someone else in the room." She grabbed his hand and held on tight. "But the woman must be our main priority. Come on." She strode into the room next door. A giant spider-web was set up in the center of the room, and the woman was attached to it, bound by her hands and feet. A figure lay on the floor.

"Is he…"

"Daniel." She turned his face back to hers with her hand. "Focus for a moment." Her eyes flashed determination. "The man on the floor has a cut on his head. I think he stumbled and fell. He seems drunk. He needs medical attention, but we need to look after this woman first. We have to deal with her *first*."

"Of course." What was she going on about? Obviously the woman needed their attention urgently.

"Daniel." She gripped his upper arms. "The man is Cain."

"Cain?" All ideas about seeing to the woman first evaporated with her words. Daniel tugged away from her grip and ran to the man on the floor, for the first time getting a clear view of his brother's face. "Cain!" He paced a palm flat on his brother's chest, feeling the rise and fall through the overwhelming panic washing over him. A buzzing sound was in his ears, a metallic taste in his mouth. "He's not moving," he said over his shoulder. "You're a doctor, do something." He leaned close and spoke into Cain's ear. "Cain, it's me. Can you hear me?"

Cain's eyelids flickered. "Dan…iel?" his voice was slurred. The stench of alcohol was overpowering as he spoke. "What?" his eyes opened, revealing an unfocused, glassy gaze. Then he paled, his eyes closed again and he was out.

"I need your help over here."

Kathryn was behind the woman on the web. She'd unbound both of the leg restraints, and was working on the buckle holding one of her arms in position. Daniel stood—

forcing himself to leave his brother's side.

"Hold her."

Mechanically, obediently, he did as she asked, wrapping his arms around the unresponsive woman, holding her up as Kathryn loosened first one constraint then the other. When she was free, he picked her up.

"Place her on the bed."

As he did so, Kathryn opened the bag she'd brought from her wardrobe. She pulled out a stethoscope and placed it on the woman's chest. "She's breathing. But her pulse is thready." She checked the woman carefully. "There are marks on her neck." She pointed at a small pattern of dark bruises on the woman's pale skin.

"Strangulation?"

"Perhaps. I don't know. Max found them. I think she's in shock. We have to call an ambulance."

Our father throttled our mother.

Daniel's jaw was clenched so tight he feared his teeth might shatter. "I'll handle it."

*****

Calling for an ambulance, taking the woman and Cain to hospital, was out of the question. Cain was recognizable worldwide; his face had graced every newspaper and money magazine over the past couple of months. And the woman's injuries would cause a sensation if news of them—or, God forbid—a photograph, made the newspapers.

Leaving Kathryn, he stepped into the corridor. Max had gone. Presumably doing what Kathryn had asked. He walked to the security guy a flight down. "Get Jackson up here." As the man complied, he considered his options.

A British hospital would have to alert the British police. If the woman didn't pull through Cain could be looking at assault charges, or worse. He rubbed his eyes. Blood was thicker than water, and his job—his mission—must be to protect his brother at all costs. No matter what he'd done. This had to be handled carefully. Discreetly.

He called his ex-boss. "Sergei."

"Daniel." He heard soft music and the murmur of voices in the background—Sergei must be entertaining. "It's late, have you a problem?" No censure in Sergei's tone, just curiosity.

"I'm in England and I have a situation." Sergei deserved his honesty. "I have to get Cain out of the country to France immediately."

"One moment, I'm finding somewhere more private." The sounds faded as Sergei left the room. "Okay. I am alone. Has he killed someone?"

Shocked, Daniel was unable to respond for a moment. Sergei had met his brother on numerous occasions. Did he think that his brother was really capable of such a thing? "No." His voice was clipped, his answer terse. "But it does concern a woman. She has been injured. I need…"

He'd cleaned up messes for Sergei in the past. Balanced across the line between legal and illegal like a tightrope walker without a net.

"I know what you need," Sergei said. "The plane is at a small airfield outside London. Fairfield. Your replacement is damned unreliable, I doubt I can rouse him at such short notice." Daniel knew the destination well.

"I'll fly it myself."

"I'll get the plane fueled and arrange my medical team to meet you there and accompany you to France. I presume you're going to your house…"

"Yes." Relief filled Daniel at Sergei's words.

"Vadim will telephone you on this number and pass on the details of the people we use in France for medical emergencies. Call them, tell them I sent you, and they will organize everything you need to convert part of the house into a makeshift hospital. They are discreet—no authorities will be alerted."

"Thank you." The words were inadequate, but heartfelt.

"Call me tomorrow and let me know how everything is, yes?" Sergei's voice was warm. "Your brother is lucky to have you looking out for him."

"He's blood." The thought that Cain had intentionally hurt someone was abhorrent, but right now he couldn't think about that, couldn't let the idea that his brother had somehow become just like their father consume him. He had to deal with the crisis first, deal with the consequences after. *Triage.*

"Tomorrow, then."

"Yes. Tomorrow." He terminated the call with Sergei as Jackson approached, taking the stairs two at a time.

"What is it, boss?" Zach Jackson had previously worked for Sergei's security team, but had made the move when Daniel did—seduced by the opportunity to head up a security detail.

"We have an injured guest," Daniel said. "She needs medical attention."

"You want me to call an ambulance?" Jackson asked.

"Contact the helicopter pilot. I need a helicopter that can handle a stretcher to fly us to Fairfield airstrip. I want you and the security team to stay here, Zach. Close the shutters in the house. When the helicopter arrives, I want everyone corralled downstairs so we can go without being seen. Your job is to see this party through, and to keep the house secure."

"Miss Hazzard…"

"Miss Hazzard will be coming to France with me."

*****

Where is that ambulance? She couldn't leave her patients—despite Cain's actions, her medical training ensured she could act dispassionately and treat him with the medical attention he needed—but the urge to talk to Daniel was strong.

She checked the woman's vitals again, concerned as she failed to rouse.

On the floor, Cain stirred.

She crouched beside him. "Cain. Can you hear me?"

He groaned. His eyelids flickered open. His eyes so familiar her heart twisted. "Who?" He cleared his throat. "Where am I?"

"The party. You're at the party in my house." How she could continue to live here, surrounded by the memory of finding a guest in such a state was beyond her. But it was still her house. Right now, two million wasn't near enough for the defilement it had suffered.

He touched the cut on his head. "I…my head hurts."

"You got off lightly." She could barely stand to look at him. "After what you did, I want to kill you."

He frowned. Managed to push himself off the floor to a sitting position. Then saw the woman. His eyes widened and a look of horror contorted his features. "Jesus, what happened?"

"You strangled her into unconsciousness. The police…"

At a noise from the door, she turned. *Daniel.*

He stalked over to his brother. "What the hell happened, Cain?" His voice was tightly controlled, but the hint of menace was easily discernable.

"I don't...I don't remember." A lock of dark blond hair tumbled over his forehead as he stared down at the floor. "I remember coming into the room—but after that..."

"Convenient." *The lying bastard.* Kathryn's hands curled into fists. She breathed in and out in an attempt to keep control. "The police will doubtless piece together the missing fragments for you." She turned away from him to Daniel. "How long before the ambulance gets here? We need to get this woman to hospital."

Daniel stood. Stared at her with a look in his eye that made her blood chill. "That's not going to happen."

Chapter Thirteen

"What?" she whispered. "I don't understand. What are you saying?"

"We are moving her and Cain out of here. The helicopter will be here shortly to take us to an airstrip where we'll board a plane to France. She'll have the best possible care—no expense will be spared—"

"No way." She jumped up from the floor, and stood in front of the bed, protecting the woman like a Rottweiler. "I'm a doctor. You can't transport an unconscious woman out of the country. We don't even know who she is—if she came here with a friend or alone. She needs medical attention."

"She has medical attention." He turned her own words back on her. "She has you."

"Explain to me…"

"Taking her to hospital now means the police will be involved. They'll investigate, and details of the party are bound to make their way into the newspapers. Do you want that? For your house to be identified as the location for a sex party? A debauched sex party where a woman was hurt?"

"This woman's health is more important than

anything." Her gaze flickered to the man who still sat, dazed, on the floor. Daniel stood next to him, protecting Cain like a guard dog. Showing solidarity with a brute. "But it's not about me, or my house, is it? It's about him." She extended a shaking finger. "You're trying to protect your brother, aren't you?"

She'd slept with him. Had screamed as he brought her to orgasm, again and again. Had given herself willingly to a man with no sense of right and wrong. No moral code. *What a colossal mistake.*

"I couldn't have hurt her…" Cain muttered weakly. "I don't remember. Why don't I remember?"

Daniel placed a hand on Cain's shoulder, aligning himself squarely in Cain's camp.

"I'm calling an ambulance." She started across the room to the telephone, but Daniel got there first. "No. You're not." He gripped her upper arms. "Go to your room. Change. Pack a bag. When that helicopter arrives you will be on it."

*****

He didn't expect her to comply. He expected her to fight.

She surprised him. She stood still and stared at him with a look that would shatter ice. "You're not giving way on this, are you?" Her voice was quiet.

"No, I'm not. You're coming with us to make sure she is properly taken care of. But we're not taking her to an English hospital."

"You have to take her to the nearest hospital. I don't care about my reputation, or the reputation of my house. I won't have someone's health at risk. Let me make the call."

"You signed a confidentiality agreement not to talk about this evening—don't you remember?" His voice was icy and deliberate. "If you fight me on this, not only will you never see a penny of the rest of the fee for this evening, but I'll also sue you for violating our agreement. Believe me, I'll make sure my lawyer doesn't play nice." Threatening her was abhorrent, but he had to stop her talking. Had to protect Cain.

"Fine." She tugged her arms away and took a step back. Her mouth tightened and she looked down at the ground.

"I'll be back in a moment," Daniel said to Cain. If she was alone she might take things into her own hands and call the emergency services anyway.

He followed her from the room.

"Don't you trust me?" Barely banked anger bristled in her tone.

"I'm just being careful." He stood in the doorway as she dragged a small suitcase from the bottom of the wardrobe and started to take clothing out of drawers. "You should bring some clothes she can wear too. A nightdress or a robe."

She stacked the clothes into the bag with shaking hands. Then turned to him. "I need to dress."

"Go ahead."

"Turn around."

For God's sake. He'd seen every inch of her naked, most recently mere hours ago. "Don't be stupid."

Her eyes flashed. "Turn around, Daniel. I have no desire to strip in front of you." The *ever-again* didn't need to be said—he got it from her body language alone.

With an exhalation of breath, Daniel turned his back to her. She was angry, he got that. And she had a right to be—in ideal circumstances, the woman should receive medical attention at the soonest opportunity.

But he couldn't risk Cain. Looking after Cain was more than a job, it was a vocation. He hoped to hell Cain hadn't been to blame for the woman's injuries, hoped against hope that there might be some other explanation, some mitigating factor that he hadn't considered to explain away what had happened in that room.

Even if there wasn't, if Cain came clean and confessed, he still needed to be protected. If a latent violent gene had made a sudden appearance, it wasn't Cain's fault. The amount of alcohol and possibly drugs that were in his system could have caused some type of break from reality. Since he and Ben had sold the company, they'd been in non-stop party mode. The sex party was the pinnacle of their excesses, but not the only one.

Ben. I have to talk to Ben.

"I'm ready," Kathryn said.

He accompanied her back into the room. Asked Zach to keep an eye on them—emphasizing that she should not be allowed to call anyone—and went in search of Ben.

Downstairs, it was as though the horror upstairs had never happened. The party was in full swing, couples and small groups of revelers were everywhere, enjoying everything that Hazzard had to offer. The portraits on the wall seemed to look down at him with anger and disgust in their painted eyes. As though he'd defiled their home.

The girl who'd propositioned him earlier was lying on the sofa with a man between her thighs. Her mouth curved in a smile as she saw him, and she licked her top lip lasciviously in carnal invitation. He shook his head and turned away.

Sex. Bible thumpers heralded it as the cause of all evil,

and tonight, he was beginning to think that maybe they were right. His gaze darted left and right, searching for Ben in the throngs of people. *There.* Ben was lounging on a chair in the corner, and for the moment at least, he was alone. Daniel walked over, pulled up a chair, and started to talk.

*****

Kathryn asked the security guy to come in and keep an eye on Cain and the woman for a moment. Before Daniel whisked her away to France, she needed to find Max. She found her in the small, private office in the west wing.

As instructed, Max had changed her clothes, and was wearing jeans and an oversized sweater. The filing cabinet was open, and she was seated at Kathryn's desk poring over paperwork. She looked up at Kathryn's entrance. "I've found her name." She lifted a page from the desk. "Susan Merchant."

The list of guests supplied by the club had photographs of the attendees, together with mobile phone numbers, but no further information. The picture of a smiling woman in her twenties stared back at Kathryn from the page. Susan Merchant looked different, much younger and more innocent in her everyday clothes, but Max was right, it was definitely her.

"Do we know if she came alone or with a friend?"

"She arrived in one of the limousines, but she entered the hall alone—I gave her a cloak."

Kathryn sank down onto a brown leather chair on the other side of her desk. "I'll need you to run things for me for a while. Daniel is taking her to France for medical treatment."

Max started to speak, but Kathryn held up a hand to stop her. "I know. I don't agree with him for a moment—

that woman should be in hospital, not being transported over the sea, but I don't have a choice in the matter. I have to go with him—have to make sure she gets the medical attention she needs. You have to stay here and make sure that the guests are looked after, and lock up the house when they leave. I'll call you and keep you informed of developments as soon as I can."

"But when she wakes up…" All the color seemed to leach out of Max's already-pale face. "She'll be upset that she's in a foreign country—she could sue Daniel, could sue you."

"We'll worry about that when it comes to it. I have no doubt Daniel will make her an offer she can't refuse. He's good at that." Bitterness struck deep. Her own ideals and thoughts about prostituting her home had been overcome in a matter of hours, hadn't they? And Daniel would no doubt pay anything to keep his precious brother out of the reach of the law. "We don't know if there are people waiting for her to come home tonight. At best, they won't worry about her until tomorrow evening. I hate the thought of someone worrying about her." She put her head in her hands. Clenched her eyes tight shut. This evening was such a nightmare.

"I will find her address, and see if I can learn anything more about her. If she lives with someone…" Max's voice was shaky. "Don't go. I need to talk to you. I have to…"

The door opened. "There you are." Daniel stood in the doorway. "Security has closed the shutters and shown everyone into the drawing room. The helicopter is here. It's time to go."

Chapter Fourteen

The next few hours passed in a daze. They travelled from Hazzard to Fairfield, where they were ushered onto a private plane fully equipped as an air-ambulance.

Two more doctors accompanied them on the trip, both experienced in transporting injured patients. Kathryn focused on providing Susan with the best possible care during the trip, and let one of the other doctors keep an eye on Cain. As a doctor she had to provide medical assistance, no matter what her personal thoughts, but it was a relief to hand that duty on to someone else. Someone who wasn't seething with anger at the patient's actions.

Daniel was in control in the cockpit with a co-pilot at his side, so she didn't have to deal with him either.

She checked Susan's vitals again. No change.

Thoughts crowded in—ones she couldn't control—of the evening and its ramifications.

Returning to her home, to her old life, was unthinkable. Being with Daniel, rediscovering the connection that she'd felt, equally so. In one night, her life had changed totally. The sands had shifted under her feet, propelling her into a strange world where nothing was certain, everything was unknown.

If I could turn back time. But she couldn't. This new reality would have to be dealt with, sooner or later. "I'm going to rest for a while," she said to the doctor, before walking to one extra wide leather seat and sinking onto it.

"Can I get you something to eat? Something to drink?" an air attendant asked.

She hadn't eaten for hours, and needed to keep her strength up. "Maybe a sandwich or something."

The woman nodded. "Something to drink with that?"

"Some coffee. No…tea."

She turned her head away, vaguely aware that the attendant had moved on, leaving her alone again. Breathed out, for what seemed like the first time in forever. He'd threatened her. Not with violence, but with what he no doubt thought was the most effective tool that he had for doing so, the threat of non-payment of the fee for the evening.

He probably thought she gave a damn.

The most important elements had been taken care of. She'd paid the outstanding taxes, and arranged for the repair of the roof—two urgent matters that she'd had no hope of dealing with prior to meeting him. The rest of the money was just the frosting on the cake, and she'd lived her entire life so far without frosting. She didn't need new cars, didn't need long-term security. Sure, it would be nice, but she didn't need it.

What she needed was someone she could rely on. Someone who was straight, and honest, and would care for her unconditionally. She glanced over at Cain, who sat next to a doctor across the aisle.

Daniel cared for his brother—that much was evident. But protecting him from this was wrong. He should be made to face the consequences of what he had done. If Susan didn't recover—if she never regained consciousness, what then? Would Daniel try to force her to keep silent forever?

Just how far would he go to ensure her silence?

She shivered, and wrapped the blanket the air-hostess had dropped on the seat next to hers around her. Closed her eyes. An ache in her stomach spread up her torso, clutching around her heart. She'd taken him at face value. Had been seduced by his looks, and by the electric effect his body had on hers. But she didn't actually know him. Hadn't understood what drove him, what the core of the man was capable of, until this evening.

She'd made one hell of a mistake, falling for the shallow surface of a man without knowing more. Now that surface had been stripped away, and all the things that she'd been so attracted to, the soul deep connection that she'd imagined she'd felt were revealed to be nothing more than smoke and mirrors.

A powerful illusion, but an illusion nonetheless.

"*Mademoiselle?*"

She opened her eyes.

The air-hostess stood in the aisle with a tray.

Kathryn flicked down the table clipped up against the seat in front, and forced a smile. "How long before we land?"

*****

By the time they reached his Provencal home, pink-streaked dawn was breaking. There hadn't been a moment alone with Kathryn throughout the entire trip. He'd managed to force out thoughts of her as he piloted the plane, but it had been more difficult in the drive from the small French airfield. She'd refused point blank to accompany him, instead joining the other doctors in the private ambulance.

Even now, she stuck to Susan's side like glue.

She's tired. He sat in the back of the car and watched as she climbed from the ambulance and walked alongside the stretcher into the house. Fatigue was evident in the stiffness of her gait, the way she brushed back hair from her face and kneaded the nape of her neck.

Admiration for the woman—for the doctor—for everything she was swelled up inside. Her principles meant something to her—even when he made that empty threat of withholding the rest of her fee, she hadn't abandoned them. If there had been a chance of getting Susan to hospital, a chance of thwarting him, she would have done it—without caring about the consequences.

He was pretty sure she'd go to jail if she had to.

The driver opened his door and, heart sinking, he left the car and followed her.

The medical team Sergei had recommended had done an excellent job in the time available. The downstairs sitting room had been cleared, the antique rugs had been rolled up and removed, and sterile linoleum had been laid over the fine parquet floor. They had imported an impressive array of medical equipment, and brought in a hospital bed.

The doctors transferred Susan from the stretcher to the bed, and handed over their charge to a French doctor.

Kathryn started talking to the doctor, then frowned. She glanced around, and when she found Daniel, she waved him over. As he reached her side, he breathed in her familiar scent, and fought the urge to touch her. An unfamiliar jolt in his chest was unexpected at the look in her eyes. Bruised. Hurt. There for a moment, then quickly hidden.

"I want to make sure the doctor understands everything. Can you translate?"

Her husky voice made his senses stir. He wanted to be alone with her. To explain what had happened, why he acted the way he had—why Cain was so important that he'd force her to leave her home, her country, in order to protect him.

But now wasn't the time.

"Of course." Forcing himself to be as detached as she was, he turned to the doctor, and relayed the information Kathryn fed him. Despite the fact that this was much more than a case to her, her narrative was brief, detailed, and to the point.

"We have set up a separate area for your brother in the next room," the doctor informed him in French. "A nurse will be with him for the next twenty-four hours, monitoring him closely. His momentary lack of consciousness is a concern."

"And the woman?" They would have to contact her family soon—he hadn't thought past the immediate need to remove both her and Cain from the scene, and now the possible problems made his head ache.

The doctor glanced over. Another medical professional was hooking her up to a machine. "It is too early to say. An ECG will tell us a lot about her brain activity. Monsieur Vonet is a neurologist. When he has completed his analysis we should know more." The doctor's mouth pursed. "Lack of oxygen…" he frowned, "it is a shame we do not know more about what exactly happened, for how long she was deprived."

Daniel nodded. From Kathryn's report to the doctor, Cain hadn't remembered any more about the events of the night. "And my brother—will his memory come back?"

The doctor shrugged. "The doctors on the plane took a blood sample to check his alcohol levels which we will run now. If his memory loss is due to the blow to the head, there is a possibility that it may return, but if it was alcohol induced, I fear it will not." He glanced across the room to the unconscious woman, obviously keen to rejoin his patient.

"Thank you, Doctor." Daniel shook the doctor's hand, then turned to Kathryn. "Susan is being cared for. You look as though you are about to drop. Come with me."

*****

Daniel led her though the old farmhouse. Thick, white walls dulled all sound. A chill was in the air as they ventured further into the house's heart. Under her feet were old, dull, wooden floorboards. The house smelled slightly musty, as though it had been shut up for the summer.

"I called the housekeeper and asked her to make up a few rooms. We'll have to wait a few hours for breakfast until the stores open," he said.

Too tired to bother answering, she nodded.

He pushed open the door to a room, and placed her small suitcase on a bench at its foot. "You and I need to talk." His voice was urgent. "About tonight. About the way things turned out."

"I don't want to talk to you, Daniel." Her voice sounded flat, devoid of all emotion. "I'm tired."

He held her upper arms, turned her to him. "I never thought that when I brought you here it would be under these circumstances." He looked at her mouth. "I thought we'd be happy—that I'd be bringing you to my room. To my bed."

She made to protest, but he touched her mouth with his fingers, stilling her words.

"I know that won't happen tonight. You're exhausted—and so am I. I know you're angry, that you're upset. But we need to talk tomorrow. You and I..." He raked a hand through his hair. "I can't let it be over."

"It is."

He shook his head slowly, side to side. Fire blazed deep in his eyes, a fire she couldn't address, and had no chance of reciprocating. She felt hollow, dead inside. Too exhausted to even turn her phone back on and place a call to Max. That would have to wait. *Everything* would have to wait, even this conversation.

"Goodnight, honey."

Before she could move away, he brought his mouth to hers and kissed her—gently, tenderly. As though he actually cared about her.

An illusion. A very convincing, but totally fake illusion.

Chapter Fifteen

She hadn't turned her head away from his kiss, but she hadn't responded either. Her arms hung at her sides—making no move to either draw him close or push him away. She acted as though he was dead to her.

So he'd done the only thing he could, under the circumstances. He'd walked away. Perhaps after a few hours sleep she'd be more receptive, would be more capable of listening, of understanding his reasons.

He strode through the house, and pushed open the door to outside. The day hadn't started to heat up yet, but the sharp bite of the sirocco was in the air. He breathed in the scent of the lavender that bloomed under the olive tree, and sank down on the slatted wooden chair set up under its shade. Every time he came back here, he was keenly aware of the scents of the place, the chirping chatter of cicadas hidden in the trees and the undergrowth. The ambience of Provence hit like a hammer every time he returned, and for the first few hours his senses were assaulted, wooed by her beauty.

In hours, it would fade. The sounds and smells would become part of the scenery—he'd become used to them, and they wouldn't even register as part of his reality.

His eyelids closed, and he slowly breathed in the dry air, letting it fill his lungs and allowing his mind to go blank. Allowed himself to live in the moment, to force out the thoughts and worries of the present, and just live in the now.

One moment.

Then he opened his eyes, stood up, and walked back inside. He strode down the corridor back to the makeshift hospital. Pulled up a chair next to Susan, and listened as the doctors explained the results of her ECG scan. In this waiting game he had nowhere else to be but here by her side.

*****

When she woke, Kathryn was disorientated. White cotton sheets were cool against her naked skin, and the room was unfamiliar. She picked out a sound in the air, crickets, maybe?

France. The memories flooded back in a rush—a kaleidoscope of fractured images bombarding her. The woman tied to the spider-web. Cain lying unconscious on the floor, the flight, the house, the touch of Daniel's mouth against hers.

She reached for her watch on the bedside table. *Eleven*. She'd been asleep for hours, should have set an alarm. She threw back the coverlet and swung her legs to the floor. Her head was still groggy, and her body felt grimy from the night before so she walked across the room to the adjoining bathroom.

As the water streamed over her body, her mind, against her will, returned to Daniel. Last night, she'd need comfort, needed to escape the horror of what happened. He'd offered it, but she couldn't take it. Couldn't take comfort, or anything else, from Daniel Hunt ever again.

Although she'd taken his brother's money.

The thought put a bad taste in her mouth. Accepting the money now felt like complicity, felt as though she was okay with what they'd done—spiriting a woman out of the country to save a man who didn't deserve mercy. No-one deserved mercy after doing what he'd done.

She stepped from the shower and reached for a towel, decision made.

Dressed in some of the new clothes she'd brought, and feeling decidedly more human after the shower, she followed the smell of coffee to the kitchen.

The doctor sat at the table nursing a mug of coffee and a croissant. "Good morning," he greeted her. "There's coffee in the pot, and croissants on the counter."

"Thanks." She poured herself a cup, and loaded a plate with the pastry. "How is she?" Pulling up a chair, she sat opposite him.

"She's going to be okay." He rubbed a hand through his hair, tiredness evident. "She revived a couple of hours ago. There doesn't seem to be any lasting damage."

Muscles she hadn't even realized she was holding taut and tight relaxed. Relief flooded her. "Is she awake now?"

He shook his head. "She's sleeping. I've been trying to get Mr. Hunt to take a few hours rest, but he's still with her."

"Has he been there all night?" She'd presumed that after he left her he would have gone to bed too.

"Yes. Since she arrived."

"You should get some rest," she said. "You must be exhausted."

The doctor nodded. "A new medical team has arrived

to relieve me. Mr. Hunt has allocated me a room—I'm heading there now." He pushed back his plate, and stood. "I shall see you later."

"Sleep well, doctor." *He should have woken me. Should have told me.* She broke the croissant into tiny pieces, slathered it with butter, and ate. But she'd been so exhausted the previous night she'd been barely able to string two thoughts together—so she couldn't blame him for letting her sleep. Now, she was fresh, rested and ready for anything.

She drained her cup and stood.

The room they'd fitted out with medical equipment was quiet. A doctor and two nurses worked on the other side of the room, filling out paperwork and examining the patient's chart. The color had returned to the cheeks of the woman lying in the bed. Daniel sat in a chair by her side. He was awake, but the dark circles under his eyes telegraphed his tiredness.

On seeing her, he walked to her side, casting a glance at Susan as he did so. "Let's talk," he whispered, taking her arm and propelling her to the window some distance away. "She woke up."

"I heard."

His eyebrows rose.

"I met the doctor in the kitchen."

He nodded. "Yes. We have a new team now, he's taking some time out—going to sleep."

"As you should," she said, aware of the concern in her voice. He was pushing himself too far; nobody could stay awake indefinitely. "Why don't you go and sleep for a while too?"

"I won't be able to." His gaze locked with hers. "Not with this between us." He looked back at Susan. "She's going to be okay."

"The doctor said." The news had been so welcome, but didn't change the fact that he had diced with a woman's life—just to save his brother from the consequences of his actions. "That doesn't change anything though, Daniel. You still risked her life in an attempt to protect your brother." Her hands curled into fists. "Was she able to tell you what happened? Did she talk about Cain?"

His mouth flattened into a flat line. "Wouldn't you risk everything for someone you love? Someone you care about?" When she remained silent, he continued. "I had to act quickly and made the only one I thought possible at the time. You see Cain as a multi-billionaire, spoiled, rich kid. Someone who has everything, and as a result, expects that he can get away with anything and everything; that he is above the law. He isn't like that. I wish you could have known him before. Cain is…" He rubbed the back of his neck and his forehead creased as he searched for the right word. "Cain is good. He's innocent and trusting, despite what he's been subjected to in life. Our upbringing wasn't good. The man who fathered us was a complete bastard. He hurt Cain."

"And you?" A vice squeezed around her heart.

"And me," he agreed. "But I was older, and the moment I could leave, I did. While I was in the house he and I fought—physically fought. He was a cruel man, and he used to abuse our mother. After they divorced, my mother married again. I guess she wanted to put her past behind her—her new husband certainly didn't want to be saddled with a family. So she paid for me to study to become a pilot, and put Cain in boarding school. I thought he was safe. Our father had never shown Cain any aggression." He crossed his arms. "I left him." The words were damning, and he obviously knew it. "I never should have."

"What happened?"

"He slipped further into alcoholism. I don't know why Cain didn't call me—didn't tell me—I guess he was afraid. He was only sixteen." His eyes blazed as they stared into hers with the intensity of a laser. "If he strangled Susan, it was because during his holidays from school he'd been brought along to the brutal sex sessions that my father had with the local hookers. He'd had to watch that bastard…"

Words, too difficult to speak, refused to be spoken.

The pain in Daniel's face, the obvious agony he felt for what his little brother had been forced to endure was too difficult to see without reacting. Kathryn stepped closer and slid an arm around his waist.

He turned into her, gripping her shoulders tight. "I'm not looking for your pity."

Pity was the last thing she was feeling, being so close to him again. "But maybe my understanding?" Her voice sounded husky. "You feel you have to protect him. That you owe him." For the first time, Daniel's attitude to his brother made sense. Compelled by guilt, driven by duty, confused by love.

Confused by love.

She didn't love Daniel, she couldn't—it was too soon, she didn't even really know him—but the feeling welling up inside was different to any other emotion she'd experienced before, and it sure was confusing.

She cared. About the torment the man who had given him and Cain life had put him through. She understood—if she had a sibling and someone had hurt them so badly, she may well feel the same as Daniel did. But putting someone else at risk to save them…

"Where is your father now?"

Daniel pulled away from her. "He died the day of our mother's funeral."

Kathryn turned at a noise from the doorway to see Cain staring at the woman in the bed.

"She's awake."

Chapter Sixteen

Kathryn dashed to Susan's bedside. She was staring across the room at Cain's pale face, but there was no fear in her gaze, no recognition.

"Susan." Kathryn pitched her voice low and calm. She pulled up a chair and sat next to the bed. "I'm Kathryn. I'm a doctor."

Susan turned her head.

"Do you remember what happened to you?"

Susan placed her palm over her throat. "I...I remember." Her voice was faint. Her gaze flickered to the table next to the bed. To the water jug. "Can I have some water?"

"Of course." Kathryn poured a glass, inserted a straw, and held it while Susan one sip, and then another.

Cain and Daniel sat on chairs on the opposite side of the bed.

"Someone hurt you, Susan," Kathryn said. "We found you unconscious."

"It started out as a game." Susan's hand rubbed the bruises on her throat. "I know she didn't mean to hurt me."

She? Memory pictures flashed in Kathryn's mind in a

vivid slideshow. Her pausing in the corridor, hearing a noise upstairs. Max, staggering down the corridor, shock written large on her face.

"But then when the guy joined us…"

Kathryn stared at Cain. Pointed. "That guy?"

Confusion clouded the gaze Susan directed at Cain. "No. I've never seen him before." She stared at Kathryn again. "Where am I? Does my family know where I am?"

Daniel introduced himself, and explained where she was. "Who shall we call, Susan?" He strode to a desk that had been shoved into the corner, opened a drawer and pulled out a notepad and a pen. "Once you are recovered, we can arrange to get you home."

Panic was eating Kathryn alive. She hadn't heard from Max since they'd climbed aboard the helicopter—she hadn't had her phone on—maybe Max had been calling.

"Excuse me, I have to check something," she announced to the room in general. Then, not waiting for a response, she stood and hurried from the room. She pressed the power button of her cell phone, and in that moment, the moment before it sprang to life, anything and everything was possible. Maybe the woman Susan spoke of wasn't Max. Maybe Max hadn't been involved and neglected to reveal that fact to her closest friend. She clung to the possibility that this was all just a misunderstanding—a mistake.

That moment didn't last long.

Once the phone was on, voicemail notifications appeared. All with one thing in common. The sender. Kathryn scrolled to the first one and checked the time it had been recorded. Last night, before they'd even left England.

Max's voice was full of strain. "Katie—" she hadn't called her Katie for years—"I wanted to tell you before you left, but everything happened so quickly…" She paused, and Kathryn imagined her swallowing. "The woman on the spider-web; she was with me. I was the one with her—I strangled her…" She started to sob quietly. "I never meant to hurt her. Cain wasn't involved—call me back as soon as you get this. I'm sorry. I'm…" Her voice broke over the words. "I'm so sorry." The line went dead.

*****

Susan had been through a lot. So even though he wanted to question her further, Daniel forced himself to hold back—to deal with her concerns, which right then involved calling her family and friends and letting them know where she was. She didn't tell them about the sex party, about the fact that she was in France, but instead she said she was away for a few days with friends and would call when she was back.

On one thing though, she was adamant. She didn't know Cain, and hadn't even registered seeing him before. The release of pent-up emotion on hearing her words had been overwhelming, and from the look of Cain's face, he was feeling it too. Daniel had noticed Kathryn's departure, but hadn't given much thought to where she was going.

Once Susan had contacted her family, her strength seemed to desert her. Her eyes closed, and instantly, she was asleep.

"It is normal," the doctor assured them. "Her body has been through such a lot, she needs to sleep. You can question her further when she awakens."

Daniel nodded. "Cain and I will be outside. Call me if you need to."

Outside, under the shade of the olive tree, they sat. "You thought I'd done it, didn't you?" Cain asked in a soft voice. "You thought I'd hurt her."

Much as he wished he could deny it, he couldn't. "You were very drunk." The words sounded like an excuse—and they were, an excuse for believing the worst about his only remaining flesh and blood. "You and I have both been exposed to some bad stuff—stuff that leaves a scar on your soul."

Cain's jaw tightened. "I'm not like him. I've never been like him." His hands curled into fists.

Daniel gaze fixed on his brother's. They'd never spoken about what happened the day of their mother's funeral. Had never spoken about their father's death. Now, so many years later, wasn't the time to either. "Neither of us is like him." Their father had had a black soul. He hadn't cared about anyone, about anything. Neither of them had inherited that trait. "I'm sorry I considered the thought for a moment." Daniel rubbed the ache blooming in his forehead. "But you considered it too. Didn't you?"

Cain's eyes darkened. "I didn't know what happened. I still don't—the night is a blur. When she looked at me, told me she didn't know me, Jesus, Daniel, I was so relieved."

The heavy, ornate gate to the property stuttered open—having been activated by a car outside. A moment later, a dusty old Citroën car pulled up a little distance from where they sat. A woman climbed out.

"*Salut*, Daniel!" Sophie Demarchelier, his part-time housekeeper, walked over. "And Cain, it has been too long."

The men rose and kissed Sophie on both cheeks in greeting.

"Thank you for organizing everything at such short notice," Daniel said.

"I have brought provisions." She waved an arm to the car. "Help me bring them in, and I'll start on lunch."

"I'll help you." Cain shot Daniel a glance. "You should rest."

Tiredness was kicking in, and right about now the thought of retreating into his room and lying down, relaxing his tense muscles, sounded good. Kathryn still hadn't made an appearance—he'd put her in the room next to his. "Good idea." He turned away. "I'll see you in an hour or so."

*****

She'd always considered herself brave. But the thought of talking to Max made her hands shake. She'd never had to call someone she cared for and question them about almost murdering someone.

So after listening to the first message, Kathryn had turned her cell phone off, removed her shoes, stripped to her underwear, and crawled under the bedcovers. She'd curled up like a fetus in the womb, and closed her eyes in an attempt to shut the world—to shut reality out.

Cowardly? Sure. But unavoidable. Necessary. The past twenty-four hours had been filled with too many conflicting emotions, too many ups and crushing downs—her ability to process more had fled.

So she made her mind deliberately blank, and eventually fell into an uneasy sleep fractured by dreams.

A rap on the door jerked her back to wakefulness. "Come in." Her throat was dry, her voice barely audible. She cleared her throat. "Come in."

The door opened, and Daniel entered.

Everything she'd spent the past while trying to block out returned in a rush. The accusations she'd made against his brother, the condemnation she'd fired at him for wanting to keep Cain from justice. She'd been wrong—so wrong.

He walked over, removing his jacket, and shedding his shoes. His head shook from side to side at the look that must be on her face. "Shhh…" he murmured. "Don't speak." He peeled off the rest of his clothes, leaving just his black boxer shorts. She pulled back the cover and moved to make room for him in the narrow bed.

He climbed in. "Let me…" He stretched out his arm, and she scooted close, resting her head at the place where his chest and shoulder met. His arm curved around her back, not pulling her closer, but resting on her bare skin. The warmth of him—the scent of his skin, and the light brush of his fingers against her shoulder filled her with a zen-like feeling of perfect rightness. His heart beat steadily under her ear. She should talk to him about Max—should stop being a coward, and actually ring Max back and learn the whole truth. But right now—right now, enjoying this moment of calm and oneness was paramount.

His other hand smoothed over her temple. Stroked her cheekbone, then traced her jaw. Finally, he tilted her mouth up to his. "I've missed you." He kissed her lips in a slow and tender exploration. His tongue traced the seam of her lips and she opened to him. Except for the hours he'd spent at Susan's bedside, they hadn't been physically apart since the party at Hazzard, but mentally they'd been on the opposite sides of a battle forged in fire and responsibility. He'd been on Cain's side, and she'd considered herself on Susan's. She'd been wrong—she should tell him…

But as his arm curled around her, bringing their bodies into alignment, and moving her on top of him, the urge to confess faded as pure, unadulterated need bit.

With one hand, he expertly removed her bra and tossed it aside. The sensitive tips of her breasts rubbed against his chest, and the feeling of calm instantly morphed into something new, something vital. His hands stroked over her back, again and again. He was hard beneath her. Hard chest, rigid abs, rock hard cock.

With a sigh, she opened her legs and pressed her core against him. Angled up to sitting. His eyes were almost closed, showing a mere sliver of glittering green. His hands slipped from her back to her stomach, slid up her torso to cup her bare breasts. Her nipples peaked beneath his fingers, and when he rubbed them between finger and thumb, a flash of sensation stretched a twisted, electric rope of desire from her nipples to the juncture of her thighs.

Her heartbeat tingled there, in her wet heat. The tip of his cock, covered by soft cotton, pressed against her clit, making the need to have him inside urgent. She couldn't hide her reaction to him. Couldn't hold back the groan that escaped as he rocked his hips up.

His mouth curved into a sensuous smile. With the fingers of one hand still playing with her nipple, turning and twisting it, his other hand stroked a lazy trail to her panties. Teasing, he dipped his fingers under the waistband, then out again.

"Daniel." Her voice was husky and desperate. And obviously appreciated, as his smile widened and his cock flexed.

"Up."

She pushed her core away from him—helped him

peel off her panties, then freed him from his boxers. She curved a hand around his rigid length and slowly moved her hand up and down, earning a groan from him as her reward. *Wet.* She wanted him wet and slippery, hot and hard. A bead of moisture was on the head of his cock, but that wasn't enough, so she angled up and rubbed her wet core from his balls to his tip.

His smile disappeared. "Holy fucking shit." His fingers gripped her hips, taking back control of her movements in an instant.

She ran her hands over her own breasts. Daniel's breath caught then in a rapid and expert motion he moved her off him, and let his cock jut free to the perfect angle to enter her. *How can I live without this?* The thought struck from nowhere as Daniel thrust, deep and sure. She pushed it away—unwilling to consider that somehow he'd become so essential, so much a part of her that the thought of being without him hurt. She arched her back and matched her pace to his, breathing hard with the exertion of their frantic movements. Trailing her hands behind her bottom, she stroked the back of her fingers against his balls.

She wanted to come, needed to come.

Daniel's hand moved to rub her clit, slipping against the sensitive nub in a rapid rhythm. The sound of her breathing, the heat building in the place between her thighs, the scent of their arousal, of their lovemaking, combined into an overwhelming sensual assault.

"Scream for me, honey," he muttered. "Come for me."

His voice was harsh and clipped. He was hanging on by a hair, so close she could feel it. She needed something, something more. His eyes were closed, and the expression on his face was of exquisite pleasure-pain. It was easy to sink down, to press her breasts against his chest, to claim his mouth.

And, as his tongue thrust into her mouth, matching the movement of his cock, her inner walls gripped him hard then released, again and again, as her orgasm crested.

Daniel's arms came around her, holding her so tight it was difficult to breathe. The delicious slide of their bodies, the slam of his pelvis against her clit, the wetness where they were joined, took her higher, past the point of orgasm into a world of pure sensation, where nothing could be held back, everything had to be shared.

They were alone in this nirvana. Daniel buried his face in the juncture of her neck and shoulder, and with an inarticulate groan, spilled his passion into her.

Chapter Seventeen

He was asleep. Lying on his side, with one hand behind his head, and the other on the indent in the bed that marked the spot where she had lain mere moments before.

It wasn't surprising considering Daniel had suffered a night without sleep on top of the jetlag he was bound to be feeling from the previous day's journey to England. He hadn't stirred as she carefully raised his arm and slid from the bed. His breathing was deep and even—it was likely that fireworks could go off outside and he wouldn't hear them.

For a moment she just stood there, drinking him in. The urge to climb back into bed with him, to run her hands over the muscles of his chest, to breathe in his scent, was strong, but she had to resist it.

She picked up her cell phone from the bedside table, slipped on a robe she found hanging in the wardrobe, and walked out into the bathroom to make the call she'd been dreading for hours. "Max—it's me."

"Thank God." Relief was evident in Max's voice. "I was so worried. How is she?"

Fear at what Max would reveal choked her response

for a moment, but Kathryn swallowed and forced out the words that would open the conversation. "She's going to be fine."

Max made an inarticulate sound, as though emotion had overcome her.

"What happened, Max? What the hell happened?" Max's response wouldn't have the power to destroy the way she felt about her friend—they'd always been there for each other, and being tested like this only confirmed the strength of that. "I can forgive you everything, you know." Her voice was soft. "I just need to know. I need to know all of it."

"Susan and I met for the first time at the party. You know I don't usually go for women, but there was just something about last night, something about her, that I found impossible to resist. Before long, we were talking, then we were kissing, and when she suggested we take it somewhere more private, I wanted to as much as she did." She paused for a moment. "We went up to the bedroom, and I fastened her onto the spider-web." She cleared her throat. "You don't need a blow by blow—but after a while she encouraged me to tie the scarf around her neck. She'd done auto-erotic asphyxiation before and loved the buzz it gave her during sex."

Kathryn screwed her eyes up tight. "And?"

"And then Joel came in."

Joel? "Joel was there? I didn't know…"

"We could invite a guest, and he's a member of the Gateway Club—we'd met at the beginning of the evening and agreed we would both be free agents for the night—that we'd both experience everything the night had to offer. The scarf was around Susan's neck, and she smiled and nodded as he asked if he could join us. God, it's so hard to go over all of this—"

"Keep talking." She had to know all of it. Had to know.

"He was aroused. Totally into what we were doing, and keen to play. He told me I was a bad girl for partying without him. I couldn't tell if he was serious or not, he was different somehow, more alpha. He took charge of the situation and tied a blindfold over my eyes. While I was kissing Susan I heard him take his pants off behind me, then he gripped my hips and pressed himself against me."

She took a deep breath. "We were all carried away, completely involved with our own pleasure. When I got down on my knees in front of Susan to bring her to climax, he entered me from behind. I gripped the ends of the scarf, and she was moaning, I was…well, I lost it. I stopped paying attention for a moment, and then Susan stopped…" She broke into a sob. "She stopped moving."

"Christ." Imagining the horror of that moment made Kathryn's stomach twist.

"I ripped off the blindfold, jumped up, and loosened the scarf. She was breathing, but she'd slipped into unconsciousness. Joel had been drinking, and taking something, coke, I think. He totally freaked out and tried to get me to leave her. While I was trying to revive Susan, he left. I heard him running down the corridor heading for the other staircase."

"The back stairs." There were two staircases in Hazzard—the servants' stone staircase would allow anyone to access the rest of the house without detection. He could easily have vanished without being seen.

"Someone came in a couple of minutes later. I expected Joel. I thought he'd gone to get help, but it was

Cain. He was drunk. He rushed over to help me, lost his footing when the rug shifted on the wooden floor, and fell, hitting his head on the table."

"Why didn't you tell me this?" Cain had been blamed for something he didn't do, and didn't remember the details.

"I...I don't have any excuse. Everything happened so fast and I was so upset I couldn't get the words out. Before I knew it, Daniel had whisked you all away."

"Where is Joel now?"

"I don't know. He's not answering his cell. I want to fly out and join you—to talk to Susan and tell her how sorry I am. I want to make things right. I'm responsible for this and—"

She had resolved to forgive Max everything, but that didn't stop anger from welling up inside. A simple sorry was damned inadequate when it came to someone's life almost being destroyed.

"She could have died, or had brain damage. She might never have woken up at all. You're damned lucky, Max. You and Joel could have been looking at a murder charge."

A sound behind her. The opening of the bathroom door. "*Max* did this?"

She turned. Daniel stood in the doorway, naked. His eyes narrowed, and his eyebrows pulled together in a frown. She muttered into the phone "I have to go" and shoved the cell phone into the pocket of her robe. "Daniel, I—"

He turned, and walked back into the bedroom. She followed, distracted, despite her best intentions, by his nakedness. But not for long. The reason he'd returned to the bedroom became clear as he picked up a pair of jeans and put them on.

Half dressed, he turned back to her. "Max?" he asked again, his voice cold and his expression stony. "Just how long have you known?"

"When I came up here to sleep last night I turned my cell phone back on and there were messages. I..."

"You've known all this time and didn't tell me?"

"I had my cell off—I didn't know."

"Until you came up here to sleep." He spoke slowly, deliberately. His mouth thinned. He took a shirt from the wardrobe and shoved his arms into it. "All those hours I was sitting by Susan's bedside, waiting for her to wake up, thinking my brother had attacked her. All that time you knew..." He grimaced and started toward the door.

How could she explain that she hadn't spoken to Max until just now, that she hadn't been in full possession of all the facts, of the full truth? *But you did know.* A little voice inside whispered. Max confessed and you didn't tell.

He read the truth in her face, and she didn't deny it. Any excuse she might give would sound weak and pathetic. "She's my friend."

"And Cain's my brother. But that didn't stop you trying to bring him to justice, did it?" He opened the door and walked out.

*****

I need a drink.

Daniel strode through the house to the kitchen, filled a glass with ice, and retreated into his library. He poured a measure of Maximum Extra Anejo into the heavy crystal glass, and watched the petrol-swirl of vivid color on the drink's surface as he swirled it around before swallowing a mouthful.

Life's a bitch. A bitch with a cruel sense of humor. For

the first time in years—scratch that—in forever, he'd let down his guard enough to let a person vault over the top. To breach his defenses. Last night he'd needed her. Watching over Susan, waiting for her to wake up, he'd gone over and over the possibilities, of what would have to be done if she failed to wake. Someone would have to pay, and it wouldn't be his brother, Cain would never survive in prison.

But he would. He swallowed another mouthful of the aged rum. Back then, at Susan's bedside, he'd been consumed with how he could persuade Kathryn to perjure herself and back up the lie that Daniel had been responsible. The midnight-black prospect of a life behind bars was a nightmare he'd lived in for the hours before Susan opened her eyes.

And the rush of emotion when she discounted Cain as her attacker.

He hadn't been able to take any more after that. Not without sleep.

So he'd come to the woman he'd started to think of as his safe haven. Had squeezed every drop out of her warmth, her concern, her—what he had thought was love. In her arms, deep inside her, he'd found peace along with the passion.

I'm a goddamned idiot.

This whole thing had got messed up since he made the decision to quit flying to work for Cain and Ben. When he'd been working for Sergei life had been a hell of a lot simpler. He just flew the plane. Got paid good money for doing it, and didn't have to deal with people's problems. Being here reminded him of how things used to be. Of a simpler life. He hadn't been looking for somewhere to live when he first came across the old farmhouse with a For Sale sign hammered into the arid ground at the gate. And when the impulsive decision to drive up to the house and take a look had struck, he hadn't anticipated the feeling of peace that had filled him as he sat under the olive tree with the owner in the midday sun.

Something about the house just felt right. Owning somewhere so beautiful, so tranquil, hadn't ever been a dream of his, but that day he'd shaken hands on a deal to buy the house without a second thought.

And I'm going to sell it? He looked around the library at the book-laden shelves, the collection he'd put together over the past five years. The large, cast-iron range he'd bargained a dealer in Marseilles down for. For the first couple of years, he'd spent Christmas here alone, barricaded in the house against the elements with a fridge full of food, a pile of chopped wood to feed the fire, and a stack of books to read. Last year and the year before Cain had flown out to spend Christmas with him. They'd shopped in the weekly market—he'd even become so into cooking he'd tackled roasting goose with all the trimmings for Christmas dinner.

He'd never brought a woman here. That side of his life—the taking a woman to bed part—had always been separate. The situation with Cain and Susan had forced him to bring them here, to bring Kathryn here, and change the dynamic of his home.

At least she was staying in the spare room rather than his bed. Because he'd never be able to sleep in there again without the memories of lying there with her crowding in.

He drained his glass and put it down carefully on the small marquetry table he'd found in an antique shop in town. Smoothed his hand over the worn leather armrest of his favorite armchair. Sure, he could pack up all this stuff and ship it to a new house in America, but it wouldn't fit—it wouldn't be the same. Everything belonged right here. It fit. He fit. This wasn't just a place to lay his head, it was his home.

For the first time, he could see how Kathryn felt about her house. He'd formed an instant attachment to this place, and now, five years later, the thought of uprooting felt like he was tearing out a part of himself and leaving it here. How much more difficult would it be to leave somewhere that you'd grown up in, that your parents, and grandparents had grown up in? A place that defined both the person you were and the way you wanted to be?

He poured himself another drink. The first time he'd seen Kathryn Hazzard he wanted to have her. The compulsion to take her away for a holiday in Brazil after their first night together should have been a warning that she could become more. Could become a dangerous obsession, but the taste of her had been too addictive to deny.

He rubbed the ache blooming in his temples, felt the buzz of the alcohol coursing through his veins. When he stepped into her house for the first time the surge of electricity was instant. He'd been hard in a heartbeat, desperate to taste her creamy skin, to feel her body shiver and pulse around him. He hadn't stopped for a moment and considered beyond that moment, hadn't seen the danger.

But he damn well saw the danger now.

*****

Kathryn jumped at the sound of a knock at the door. *He's back.* Heart pounding, she jerked the door open. A stranger stood outside.

"*Bonjour.*" The woman smiled. "I am Sophie, Daniel's housekeeper. I came to tell you that lunch is ready."

"I'm Kathryn." She forced her voice steady. "Is Daniel downstairs?"

Sophie shook her head. "He has gone into the village. Lunch will be served outside."

"Thank you." Kathryn smoothed a hand over her hair. "I'll be down in a moment."

She rooted through her suitcase, and selected her favorite cotton dress, long, loose and floral. After washing her face and brushing her hair to make herself at least a tiny bit more presentable, she walked downstairs. As promised, the table under the olive tree, covered in a gingham tablecloth, was set for lunch. Cain sat at the table alone.

"We're lunching alone. Susan is asleep," he said.

Kathryn pulled out a chair and sat. *This would be difficult.*

Cain picked up a bottle of wine. "Would you like something to drink?"

"I would." She watched him as he concentrated on filling the glass. Cain was different from his brother, more boy than man, but the family resemblance was there in the curve of his mouth, the bright blueness of his eyes. "I want to apologize to you, Cain." Her mouth dried. "I jumped to a conclusion that wasn't right, and I've treated you very badly."

His gaze lifted to hers. "I didn't know what happened either. It's not your fault."

"All the same…I'm sorry." She breathed in deep. "I've been in contact with the woman who…with Max." Speaking the words was difficult, even thinking about what

Max had done was difficult. "Max was the woman who caused Susan to black out. She tried to call me—sent me texts from the moment we left the party, but my cell was off." She looked into Cain's eyes. "It was an accident. A horrible accident."

Cain frowned. "An accident that could have resulted in brain damage, or death."

"I know. I'm a doctor, remember?" Ice clutched her insides. "You blamed me." His tone was tight, and condemnation shone in his eyes. She'd been judgmental, determined to blame him for something that wasn't his fault. Unwilling to give him the same consideration that she now piled on Max, by insisting that what had happened to Susan was an unfortunate accident.

Her feelings must have been written all over her face, for Cain stopped scowling. He placed a hand over hers. "I'm glad Susan is going to be okay."

Chapter Eighteen

Kathryn retreated into the house the moment lunch was over. She checked in with the doctor, and examined Susan again, noting the small black bruises on her neck that contradicted Max's story—hadn't Max said that the asphyxiation had been caused by the tightening of the scarf? To her frustration, there was nothing to do but wait for Susan to wake up to discover more about that night.

In the meantime, she longed to know where Daniel was. How he was feeling. And whether or not there would be a chance that he would forgive her. Her mind worked over and over the possibilities, driving her insane. So after an hour or so she'd crept downstairs into his library and selected a crime paperback to distract herself.

She'd stood in the library for a moment. Breathed the hint of rum in the air. This room was different from the rest—more personal. The pictures, the ancient Persian rug, the battered leather armchair, all seemed to be items he'd selected himself.

It felt like a sanctuary. Somewhere she shouldn't be invading without invitation.

So she wandered into the bright and airy sitting

room, curled up on one end of the long sofa, and immersed herself in the story.

A sound.

Kathryn's eyes flickered open. The door, someone opened the door. She blinked. Her fingers checked the space before her on the sofa. No book, it must have fallen from her fingers to the floor. The light that had filled the room earlier had faded, and the room was in darkness. It must be night. She'd been asleep for hours.

"What are you doing in here?" Daniel's voice was near—he must have walked up to her in the darkness. "No-one knew where the hell you were." She couldn't see him, but the fact he was royally pissed was evident.

"I fell asleep. What time is it?"

"Late." He touched her ankle. Then his hand smoothed over her calf.

Electricity danced across her skin, so strong she couldn't suppress a tiny gasp. How can he affect me so much? "Did you get whatever you needed to get done?" She wanted to tell him she'd missed him—that she wanted to talk through what had happened, make things better between them, rewind the clock…

"Yes." His hand stroked around the back of her knee, then slid underneath the hem of her dress to caress her thigh.

"I want you."

"Shut up, Kathryn." His voice was rough—as though he'd come to the end of his patience. His palm was hot against her skin, his movements deliberate and masterful. He tugged her further down on the sofa, slipped his hands between her thighs in a move that left her breathless. Then his mouth was on hers, one hand was at the nape of her neck holding her in position as he plundered her mouth again and again. He tasted faintly of rum and coffee, she breathed in his scent, the sharp hint of citrus mixed with musk.

Nothing mattered more than tasting him, feeling him.

In one smooth movement, he jerked her panties down and off, and pressed his palm against her wet heat. She couldn't see him, could only feel, could only hear the harsh breaths that they both made. Sounds of need, of desperation.

Her shaking hands undid his belt, unzipped his pants, and shoved his jeans down. She couldn't resist him, couldn't deny the urge to have him enter her a moment longer. Her hips pushed off the sofa, moving from side to side to make his hand move, to make his fingers fit where she wanted him most.

When he moved his fingers over her clit, she almost lost it then and there. "Daniel," she moaned.

"Shut up." He plundered her mouth again. Then his hand moved to grasp his cock and position it at her slick entrance. Her inner muscles clenched as he held back, rubbing the tip against her clit in a teasing torment. Nothing mattered, nothing existed except the slow and sure rocking of his body against hers. *I want him inside. Shit, I really need him inside.*

She sucked his tongue. Hard. Then released it, and thrust her tongue into his mouth again and again, driving herself wild.

When his cock finally entered her, the ecstasy was so intense she couldn't help but jerk her head side to side, her body denying, then accepting every sensation.

Being fucked by him was so fucking good.

She gripped his ass as he pumped into her in a relentless rhythm, feeling every stroke against her inner walls, legs quivering as he unerringly found her G-spot.

His mouth was at her ear, at her neck, at her breast. In the blackness, he was everywhere. Her fingers gripped into the sleek muscles of his shoulders as the first stirrings of her orgasm threatened.

She wrapped her legs around his back, linked her ankles, and held him as he jackknifed in powerful thrusts a few more times, until she couldn't hold back the scream he'd once upon a time told her she should just let free.

As her inner muscles clenched around him, he shouted, fisted his hands in her hair, and raced over the cliff with her.

For long moments, the only sound in the room was labored breathing. She tried to catch her breath, unlinked her ankles, and let her legs slide back onto the sofa. The weight of his body lying on her was delicious. Making love with him was so right—so healing after the trials of today. He'd forgiven her.

She lifted a hand, touched the side of his face, feeling the brush of soft whiskers against her palm.

He jerked his head away.

Slipped out of her.

And stood. "Dinner is in an hour."

Then he walked out.

*****

Her taste was in his mouth. The memory of the sounds she made, the way she'd shown so graphically what she wanted, what she needed, and taken it, was impossible to brush off. The sex was good. The best he'd ever had. Even now, he wanted to walk back in there and do it all again—taste between her legs, and have her fingers pull his hair out at the roots.

But damn, why had she felt the need to touch his face after?

As if they were more than lovers. As if they were actually "in love".

Disgusted by his weakness, he strode into the bathroom, stripped, and stepped under the shower. Turning the flow of water up to as strong as it would go, and the heat to hot, he stood under the punishing needles until his skin reddened. Then he soaped the scent and all trace of her off his body.

Resting his head against the cool tiles, he closed his eyes.

He hadn't had anything vital to do when he left. Had just needed to get out of there, drive through the hills until his anger had dissipated. On the peak of the nearest hill, he'd climbed from the car and called Sergei to thank him for the use of the plane, and update him on events. The Russian had become more than an employer, he'd become a friend. When he drove back to the farmhouse, he was able to see the situation more clearly. He had his life. She had hers. He'd been stupid to think for a moment that they could come to some compromise, that there would be some way to dovetail two totally different lives into something that had a hope of working.

They had nothing in common. She'd been born with everything. The mansion in the country was so far from his experience of life, it might as well be a fairytale castle in the sky. The painted faces on its walls had stared down at him, a stranger passing through the house, and her life.

He turned off the water and grabbed a towel. While she was here in his house, he had no chance of resisting fucking her, but that was all it was. All it could ever be. He'd never forgive her for not telling him straight away when she'd learned of Cain's innocence.

She could like it. Or she could leave.

*****

When Kathryn came downstairs an hour later she had got herself together. She'd taken a shower and washed the scent of Daniel from her body. The way he'd been, so distant, so matter-of-fact, had fractured the feeling of closeness that had been between them. She'd been making love, but he'd been just fucking. Was this how it would be between them from here on in? If so, she didn't think she could bear it.

She'd just lain there on the sofa as he walked away. Confusion swirling inside at his detachment from what, for her, had been a magical experience. Because making love with Daniel was never ordinary, was never routine. She'd never felt like this before. The previous lovers she'd picked up in bars all around the world had never affected her the way Daniel did. Perhaps it was because she and Daniel were more than casual acquaintances—were more than fuck buddies.

She'd thought she could go to bed with him without feeling—without wanting. But she couldn't turn the clock back. She couldn't believe how wrong she'd been when she thought he made love to her with forgiveness in his heart.

Now the only question was how long she could stay here.

Her house, her home, needed her. She just walked away without looking back. All the furniture brought in for the party from the props company would, by now, have been moved out and her furniture would have been restored to its rightful place.

At least she hoped Max had overseen all those variables. But the way Max had been, so distracted and so upset about Susan, it was highly likely that chaos reigned back at Hazzard.

And she didn't care.

Now, as she walked through Daniel's silent house to the dining room, the thought of what to do and how to proceed was a conundrum without a solution. Daniel wanted her; there was no doubt about that. But he didn't trust her. His loyalty to Cain was absolute, and in his eyes, she'd threatened that. Words weren't enough.

She rubbed at her temple, then pushed open the door to the dining room.

Cain and Daniel sat at the table with a selection of cold meats and salads before them..

"Hi." Cain looked up. The corner of his mouth turned up in a gentle smile. "Susan is still asleep."

Kathryn pulled out a chair and sat down.

"Her first concern when she woke up was about her family. I know she is keen to go home as soon as possible," Daniel said. "But I have concerns about her home alone. I managed to question her a little after she telephoned her family, and discovered that she lives in a flat, and has no one to take care of her. The doctor assures me that there will be no after-effects from her strangulation, but I would prefer it if she had an opportunity to convalesce further." He kneaded the muscles at the back of his neck. His eyebrows pulled together.

"I've been busy this afternoon," Cain said. "I found a spa close to the town she lives in where she can convalesce with the added backup of a medical team on the premises. I inquired about booking her in to a suite for a week or so. I'll fly back with her and get her settled."

"There is no need for you to do that," Daniel said. "You don't even know this woman."

Cain's eyes flashed. "I know I'm responsible."

"You're not responsible, Cain. What happened was an unfortunate accident—an accident no one expected and no one wanted. If anyone is responsible, it's Max." Kathryn's heart ached as she spoke the words, but she couldn't allow Cain to take responsibility for something that wasn't his fault.

"Her injuries happened at my party." Cain's jaw clenched. "So I am responsible. Technically, I don't owe her anything, but morally...I owe her."

"I'll deal with it," Daniel said.

"No." Cain was adamant. "Your job is to make sure Ben and I aren't taken advantage of in business. Not to do everything for me. I've leaned on you for too long. You took us out of the country because you thought I'd hurt her, didn't you? To escape prosecution?"

Daniel nodded.

Cain's mouth thinned into a line. "I appreciate the sentiment, but I'm not a child. If I had been responsible, your first thought should have been to make sure Susan was okay, not to help me escape the law."

Daniel glowered. "You're my brother." Tension sparked in the air around them. "There's only you and me. I left you once when I shouldn't have and I won't again. Nothing is going to happen to you on my watch."

This was obviously a private discussion she shouldn't be listening to. Kathryn drank a glass of water and started to get up from the table. "You both need to talk—I should go."

"No," Cain said. "Please, stay, eat. This conversation is over." He glanced at Daniel. "I think we should terminate this working relationship."

"What?" Daniel's eyes blazed. "You know damn well you need me, Cain. If I hadn't been there, you…"

"I wouldn't have run, like a bloody coward."

There was a rap at the door.

"Excuse me." The doctor stood in the doorway. "Susan is awake."

*****

Susan's face was less pale, and she sat up in bed propped up by pillows.

Cain walked straight to her, and sat next to the bed. "How are you feeling?" He leaned close, with a look in his eye…as if…

Daniel blinked. As if he had *feelings* for her. Could he have? Had his brother's perceived guilt at what had happened to Susan have turned to caring about her?

Susan smiled at Cain. "I feel much better, thank you. I wanted to talk to you all about what happened."

Kathryn swallowed hard. "I've spoken to the woman who caused your injuries, Susan. Max is very upset; she tightened the scarf without realizing the damage she was doing. She asked me to apologize to you—to tell you that…"

"But it wasn't her fault," Susan insisted. "Max was blindfolded, and she was…" Her face reddened and she looked at her hands on the bed. She swallowed. "She was going down on me, and holding the ends of the scarf, tightening it, but the man…"

"Joel," Kathryn said.

"Joel. He was angry. He was fucking Max, but he was staring into my eyes, as if to tell me that she was his, not mine. And then his hands were tightening around my throat. He meant to hurt me. He wanted Max all for himself."

Cain reached for Susan's hand, and gripped it tightly. "Are you saying he did it deliberately?"

"Yes." Susan's gaze was open and honest. "He squeezed the air out of my lungs and there was nothing sexual about it."

"My God." Kathryn raised panic-laced eyes to him. "Max is in danger. She didn't know…"

"Where is he?" They needed to get a handle on this and quick. "Has Max heard from him?"

"No." He could see Kathryn shaking. "But she may have left messages for him. Oh my God, she might have told him Susan has regained consciousness."

"You can identify him," Cain said to Susan. "You're the only person who knows the truth of the situation, who knows his intent."

Daniel walked Kathryn to a chair and sat her down. He rested his hands on her shoulders. "Okay, we have to catch this man." He looked at Susan. "Don't worry, Susan. There's absolutely no way this man is getting within an inch of you again."

"I want to go home," Susan said. "I want to go back to my life."

"I've arranged for you to convalesce in the spa close to your home," Cain said. "I'll accompany you there and stay with you until he's captured."

"I'll arrange a security team to go with you when you

are ready to travel in a day or so," Daniel said.

"I'll organize a jet to take us to England immediately. We need to call Max."

Chapter Nineteen

Daniel placed a call to his security man on the ground, Zach Jackson. Quickly and efficiently, he made sure Zach increased the protection detail on Max. "He's a psycho, Zach," he explained. "We need to get the police involved."

Kathryn wouldn't like it—she was so protective of her house, of her damned reputation. She'd insisted on confidentiality, keeping this out of the newspapers could be difficult.

"Don't worry boss, I'm on it," Zach said. "She'll be safe."

With that, Daniel walked into the kitchen where Kathryn was speaking to Max on her cell. She was pacing back and forth. He walked straight to her side.

"Daniel is here," she said. "I'll fill him in." She moved the cell away from her ear and turned to him. "She still hasn't heard from him. But she left a message on his voicemail to say that Susan had regained consciousness and would be okay." Worry was evident in her eyes. She chewed on her bottom lip.

"I've spoken to Zach," he said. "Max will be safe at Hazzard."

"Shouldn't Zach take Max somewhere? Somewhere safe, where he can't find her?"

He hadn't considered the idea, but now he realized it was a good idea. "Maybe so. Ask her to put Zach on the line, would you?"

Kathryn passed on the message to Max, then handed her cell phone to him.

"Zach, change of plan. I want you to take Max to a safe house. Take the team with you."

"Should I leave someone here to keep an eye on things?"

"Yes. Leave Bill and a couple of other guys. Kathryn and I will be there as soon as we can. I called the pilot, but they won't have a plane ready until morning. Keep her safe, Zach."

He handed the phone back to Kathryn who talked to Max for a few moments more, and then terminated the call.

"We can't do anything else tonight," he said. "We should get some sleep." The last thing he felt like doing was sleeping, but they would both need all their energy for what was to come. "We have to get the police involved, and once that happens, the truth about the party will come out. The reputation of your house is going to suffer."

"There's nothing I can do about that." She faced him. "I wish we could just stay here," she whispered. "I want this nightmare to end."

"It will be over soon." *But what then?* She'd go back to her life, and okay, her reputation would be tarnished and her house would be notorious as the scene of a lurid sex party, but in time people would forget about it, and her life would return to normal.

He struggled against the urge to pull her close. Every

time he tried to walk away from her, something else happened to keep him by her side.

"I'm sorry," she whispered. "I'm sorry about blaming Cain—for not telling you about Max the moment I knew…she's my oldest friend, I didn't know what to do."

She'd protected the ones she loved. Just as he did.

Barely three hours ago she'd been in his arms, pressing her soft lips against his neck, accepting every thrust of his desperate cock into her warmth. In the darkness, it had been impossible to see her face, to make out her expression. But her hand on his face had expressively conveyed her emotions through touch alone—she'd felt more than lust for him at that moment, a lot more.

The sensible thing was to walk away — to run away from her, and not look back. Ever since she'd strolled back into the dining room dressed in black jeans that clung to her curves, he'd been unable to distance himself from her. A hint of hurt was in her eyes, a knowledge that things had changed between them for the worse. And yet, there was a war going on inside him. An urgent voice telling him he couldn't let her walk away. Couldn't face the fact that when she did it would be forever.

Shit.

Her head tilted up. He could make out golden flecks in her chocolate brown eyes. She breathed in a shaky breath. He rubbed his thumb along her jawline and watched her eyes darken, the black centers expanding.

Her mouth parted a fraction, and her head angled, as though she was a cat leaning in to his touch.

A wave of lust blindsided him, but he resisted. "Go to bed, Kathryn." It killed him to walk away.

*****

The next morning, Daniel woke early, dressed quickly and went downstairs.

Cain was in the hallway on the telephone. He muttered something, then hung up the moment he saw Daniel. "We have a problem." He frowned, and his shoulders were stiff, making him look very different from the way that he usually did. Normally, Cain was so relaxed he might as well be horizontal, but today...

"What's the problem?"

"That was Zane. One of the supermodels went to the press—details of the party are all over the news in this morning's papers."

Shit. "How bad is it?" Daniel was already on the move, walking to his laptop set up on the table in the dining room and turning it on.

Cane followed. "He says it's pretty bad. One of the British tabloids has it, and they're calling the house the House of Sin. The security guy they left at Hazzard last night is under siege, and now television has got in on the act and there are vans parked outside the house."

"What's happening?" Kathryn walked into the room, her hair hanging wet around her shoulders.

He went to her, as if standing by her side might make some difference to the news he had to deliver. "I'm sorry," he said, not knowing how to soften the blow, how to make this nightmare recede. So he simply said the words.

He turned to Cain. "You and Susan better hang tight here for a while. They'll never track you down here, and right now the last thing we need is another distraction."

"And Max? Have they identified Max too?" Kathryn asked.

Cain shook his head. "No, not yet. I'm afraid they

seem to be focusing all their attention on you."

"We need to get to England and talk to Max as soon as possible," Daniel said. "I'll have the car brought around, go get your bag."

Kathryn nodded, turned, and ran back upstairs.

"It's really looking bad, bro," Cain said. "Zane said they were digging into Kathryn's family history. They went to the hospital where she used to work and have been talking to her colleagues."

She always went to such lengths to keep her private life and her personal life apart. She'd even told him once that no one she worked with knew she lived in a stately home—that she'd wanted to be appreciated for her abilities as a doctor, rather than for her house or her pedigree. She was going to hate this.

Chapter Twenty

Booking a private plane at short notice was practically impossible, even for a multi-billionaire. Daniel guessed such men owned their own, just as Sergei did. It made no sense for Cain and Ben to own their own Learjet — the amount of times they'd need it didn't warrant the expense. And there must be many men and women in the same position, needing the occasional use of a private plane and having to navigate the confusing selection of companies offering the service on the internet.

Even though Sergei had offered, Daniel hadn't wanted to take advantage of his generosity again, so he'd found someone to supply a plane and pilot at short notice, but the service was lacking. He knew damn well just how he'd run such a business — maybe it was something to consider now he was newly unemployed.

On the flight from France to England, they read everything they could about the rising storm at Hazzard. Zack was right; the voracious press was on a feeding frenzy. Not only had journalists managed to track down doctors and nurses who had worked with Kathryn in the hospital, but also they'd found a man she'd slept with a year ago while on holiday in Corfu.

Her brown eyes had widened as the altogether too good-looking, surfer dude had told the gossip columnist live on air that he'd had no idea he was sleeping with such an illustrious stranger. "I just thought she was a regular person, you know? I met Katie at a bar, the attraction was instant, and both of us were looking for a good time. And hey, we found it!"

At that, she'd groaned and rested her head in her hands. "Oh my God."

She was in such mortified agony he'd bitten back his reaction to the jerk's revelations. He hadn't even asked her why she'd slept with a guy who looked to be in his mid-twenties, no older.

What the hell. The men she'd screwed, the decisions she'd made, were in the past. And he'd been no saint either — examining his past dating history would reveal women he'd chosen for altogether the wrong reasons. He was no one to talk.

But he didn't have to like it.

"Zane has Max holed up in a small hotel a few miles from Hazzard," he said. "We'll pick up a car rental at the airport and drive out there."

A tiny crease appeared between her eyebrows. "I won't be coming with you to see Max."

What? "I don't understand. Our priority must be to liaise with Max—find out what we can about Joel, and then call the cops in to this situation."

She crossed her hands one over the other in her lap. Straightened her spine. The corner of her mouth twitched—an involuntary response that held no humor in it. "You don't need me for that. Journalists are camped out outside my house—I have to go there."

She couldn't possibly be serious. "We can up the security, drive the journalists out. Your house will be secure. Max is your friend, she needs you. Surely, you understand that talking to Max and finding Joel must be our priority now?"

"Of course." She frowned. "But it's also important that my house is secure. I haven't been home for days—I don't even know if the aftermath of the party has been cleaned up properly. I need to get home." She crossed her arms—her entire body language screaming her intractability.

"They're going to hound you," he said. Everything in him rioted at the thought of allowing her to go to her house alone and face the barrage of camera flashes that must ensue. But he had to get to Max—had to make a report to the police. "Be reasonable."

The look she flashed him indicated she would be anything but. "I am being reasonable."

"No you're not. Come on, one ex-lover has already crawled out of the woodwork, selling his story, and by the time we land God knows what else they will have dug up. You'll have to face a lot of questions about the party, questions you won't want to answer. You can't walk in there alone, and frankly I don't have the time to handhold you through this." He'd pitched his tone low, and thought he'd made his argument in a reasonable manner, but by the look in her eyes, obviously he was wrong.

"I don't need my hand held," she snapped. "I've managed perfectly well without you for the past thirty-five years. I think I can handle the situation at Hazzard without you."

"You're being ridiculous."

At that, she stood and pushed past him into the aisle. "Where the hell are you going?"

She waved a hand in the general direction of a seat two rows up. "I don't appreciate being browbeaten. You and I aren't going to agree on this, so I don't see the point of sitting next to you for the rest of this flight." She smoothed her hands over her jean-clad thighs and started walking.

*****

God, he was beyond irritating.

Kathryn settled in to her new seat and stared out of the tiny airplane window. How could he possibly think she didn't want to see Max? Of course she did. She smoothed back her hair from her face.

But Max was safe and once they landed Daniel would be joining her too. Hazzard, on the other hand, was vulnerable and under attack. A feeling of guilt slithered under her skin like a grass snake. She hadn't given her home a thought since she'd run off to France. Okay, so she'd had no option but to run off to France—but once Susan had recovered, responsibility hadn't kicked in as it should.

Instead, she spent her time either having sex with Daniel, or fantasizing about it. She barely recognized the woman she'd become since meeting him. She pressed her palm against her breastbone, still feeling the over-rapid pulse of her heartbeat. He had no right to tell her what to do. She shouldn't really be surprised that he was so dictatorial—after all, the discussion with Cain the previous night had revealed more about Daniel than Cain.

He was a man used to taking charge. A man who thought he knew best under all circumstances. But this was her life, her house, her home, her heritage. Not his. A few sessions of spectacular, hot, steamy sex didn't give him the right to tell her what to do.

She glanced at her watch; they would land soon. The clouds from the window, instead of being fluffy and white, were grey with threatening rain. She rested her head against the cool window and closed her eyes.

Reality sucks.

"Hey."

She opened her eyes and looked over. Daniel stood in the aisle, watching her with a strange expression in his eyes. "You can't just walk away like that." He dropped down into the seat next to hers, his gaze never wavering from hers. "I care about what will happen to you if you go back to Hazzard without me. Not because I think you can't handle it—but because I don't want you to have to face that alone. When we land, I want you to come with me to see Max and then the police. Then we can go to Hazzard together."

Learning to rely on him was a mistake. And much as she wanted someone by her side as she walked into the lion's den, she had to make a stand on this, had to be strong. "You won't be here forever. I need to do this alone."

In the tight confines of the aircraft, his pure physicality, his commanding presence, dominated. He leaned in. His direct gaze was so intense it was as if he was trying to bend her to his will—force her to change her mind.

The urge to submit was strong. She wanted to rest her head against his chest and accept the strength he was offering. But sooner or later she'd have to stand alone, and now was as good a time as any.

"Please accept my decision on this." Her voice was shaky.

He just stared. She would need to be more assertive.

"I've enjoyed the time we spent together, Daniel." She gritted her teeth and forced herself to continue. "We've had fun, but both of us know we're not for keeps. My life is tied to a house in the country, and yours lies elsewhere. If the assault on Susan hadn't happened, after the spectacular night at the party we would have gone our separate ways. We both know that. I appreciate…"

Frowning, he shook his head. "We were more than a quick lay."

A band of steel tightened around her heart squeezing it and filling her with pain. She forced her voice light and casual, even though inside she felt like crying. "You saw the guy I slept with last summer, Daniel. We spent almost a week together, in bed, and out of it. I don't even remember his name." The truth was easy to confess—last summer's conquest had been a fling, he hadn't known anything about her and that was the way she'd liked it.

The unspoken inference that what she felt for Daniel was the same as she'd had for her previous fuck-buddies was laughable, but she couldn't let him know that. He had such an overdeveloped sense of responsibility, he'd stand by her side as the press ripped her and her house to shreds, offering support and being her rock.

Just as he had for Cain.

He'd do the same for anyone for whom he felt responsible. But she didn't want him by her side under such circumstances. She didn't want their relationship to be based on duty and guilt. And when he'd helped her through this crisis, he'd leave. And take her heart with him.

How did this happen? Exactly when had her feelings changed from lust to love? Love had never been on the table—had never been a possible outcome of the time they'd spent together. She wasn't even sure if this desperation that tangled her insides at the upcoming end of their relationship *was* love. Whatever it was, it wasn't healthy.

"You think you won't even remember my name?" His eyes blazed and his mouth tightened. "Don't kid yourself, Kathryn. You'll never forget it." He got up and stepped into the aisle. "But if that's the way you want it, I'll arrange a car to take you straight to Hazzard."

*****

For the remainder of the flight Daniel made arrangements. Kathryn's refusal to shelter under his protection burned, but there was little he could do about it. Zach had left one member of the security detail at Hazzard, and he placed a call informing Zach that Kathryn would be returning to the house and arranged another guard to beef up the security.

With luck, they would be able to talk to Max and the police quickly and then he could focus his attention back to Hazzard.

She said she didn't want his help. Just as his brother had. Her words were enough to make a man feel positively unwanted. Unneeded. But he couldn't just walk away.

But brute force wouldn't work in this situation—she needed time. And much as it irritated him to give it he would have to bend a little.

Tension ate away at him at the thought of her facing an uncertain reception at her family home but he shoved it down, rested his head back on the head cushion of his wide leather seat, and closed his eyes for the brief moments before they landed.

Chapter Twenty-One

Daniel made no move to touch her once they disembarked the aircraft. He walked her across the tarmac to the two waiting cars without a word.

"Will you call me once you've spoken to Max?" Despite her decision to end their relationship, half of her desperately wanted him to. Her head told her one thing, and her heart another. It was exhausting.

"I'll keep you informed." He opened the back door of the car for her. Then, as though he couldn't help himself from speaking the words, he muttered, "Keep safe."

Before she had a chance to respond, he closed her door and strode to the other car.

They'd landed in the small private airfield not far from Hazzard, and the trip home was a quick one. The narrow, country lanes became more familiar as they neared her village. Mothers pushed toddlers in strollers, ducks swam in the duck pond, and a familiar clutch of locals sat in the summer sunshine on the tables outside the pub.

Things never changed here. She was pretty sure if she'd climbed into a time machine and dialed time back fifty years, very little would have changed except the fashions of the day. Fifty years ago, another Hazzard would have been driving through the village on the way home. Fifty years from now would she still be tied to this little, emerald patch of England?

Everything inside her rioted at the thought. "Take the next left," she said to the driver. "The house is a hundred yards up on the left."

Even though she'd been told to expect it, shock thundered through her at the crowd outside the closed gates of Hazzard Hall. "Oh my God," she whispered.

She couldn't force her way through the throng of photographers to input the gate code. At their approach, the phalanx of telephoto lenses swiveled her direction.

"What do you want me to do?" the driver asked. He pressed a button on the dash automatically locking all the doors.

"I'll call the house." She rooted in her bag for her cell phone, scrolled through and dialed. *This is crazy.* Reporters crowded around the car, shouting questions. "Are you running a brothel?" "How long have you been holding these sex parties?" "Give us a statement, love!"

"Over here—smile!"

Photographers jostled each other in attempts to get her picture. Someone answered the house phone eventually. "This is Kathryn Hazzard. I'm at the gate. It's crazy here."

"Okay, we're coming down." In a couple of minutes, which seemed like hours, a black SUV raced toward the gate from the house. It screeched to a halt angling sideways. Two large men jumped out. Then the gate moved slowly inwards. The men advanced on the crowd of photographers and journalists, pushing them back.

Kathryn's driver edged the car forward. One of the

men tapped on the front passenger side window, staring at the driver through the glass.

The moment the driver unlocked the doors he climbed in. "Miss Hazzard, I am Bill Waterstone. Zach Johnson left me in charge."

The other man reversed the SUV, spun it so it faced the other direction, and started back to the house. Kathryn's driver followed.

"This is mad," she said. "All these people…"

"It's a hell of a lot better than it was earlier, Miss. This morning four journalists climbed the gate and tried to get into the house. We closed up tight once the party was over."

As they drove up outside the house she could see what he meant. Two burly guards flanked the front door. Another prowled the exterior. The heavy, mahogany shutters were fastened shut. The barricaded house looked like a fortress.

She climbed from the car and walked in through the front door. The detritus from the party had been cleared away, but the props hired for the evening still remained. She strode through the hall into the drawing room. The same was true here; her furniture was absent.

"I thought my furniture would be back." It didn't feel like home, not with the props still in place and all the items that made her house a home missing.

"Arrangements had been made to make the switch today, but…" Bill shrugged. "We decided to postpone until the press frenzy died down."

It made sense. Another man walked past the window his attention focused on the fields and woodland. But he wasn't admiring the view; he was scanning for intruders. The thought made Kathryn feel sick.

"I think I'll go upstairs." She desperately needed to

get away, to try and regain balance. This was her home yet it didn't feel like it. It felt like an alien place. She climbed the stairs, hurried down the corridor, and pushed open the door to her bedroom. Here at least everything looked the same.

She closed the door and leaned against it. *How soon can everything go back to normal?* If she just waited, it could take forever. The press was insatiable in their search for news, but crowding around her gate like this, vaulting the gate and peering through the windows was trespassing and harassment.

She knew damn well what her father would do. He'd contact the police

She sat on the bed and reached for the phone.

*****

Despite Daniel's anger at Kathryn's intransigence, worry about what she might be facing at Hazzard ate away at him. He soothed it by checking in with Bill who assured him that she was safely inside the house.

"She's tough," Bill said with admiration in his voice. "Within half an hour of her arrival, the police were dispersing the crowd. How is everything going there, boss?"

"Good. I've debriefed Max, and a couple of detectives are on their way to take a statement." He brought a written deposition with him from France, which should be enough to request an arrest warrant for Joel. "Call me if there's anything new."

He hung up, and returned to Max.

She had paled as she read Susan's deposition. Now, she sat on the sofa in the hotel suite with her hands curled around cup of black coffee. He sat next to her. "How are you?"

She gave a weak smile. "Reeling, to be honest. I had no idea that Joel did that. By now, he may well have realized that his secret is no longer secret. He would expect Susan has revealed the truth."

She frowned. "But why did he do it? I don't understand. We've been to clubs together—this wasn't our first threesome, I just don't understand why he acted as he did."

"Perhaps because you instigated an encounter without him?" Daniel suggested. "Perhaps he wants to be in control."

She considered his words for a moment, then nodded. "You could be right. All the other times he's been the one calling the shots."

"If there was a record of him behaving like this he never would have passed the Gateway Club's screening—it's very thorough."

Max's face went pink. "I…I sneaked him in."

"You what?" Daniel gritted his teeth.

Max looked at the floor.

"I know it was stupid. I just…" She rubbed her eyes. "We'd been medically screened when we visited The Gateway Club—I thought I knew him." She bit her lip. "I made an error in judgment."

It was a hell of a lot worse than that, but Daniel swallowed his anger. "When the detectives get here they need to be apprised of that fact. It's highly likely if he has done this to anyone before it won't be in the system—many people wish to keep their private sexual proclivities secret. Have you heard from him?"

"No." She picked her phone up off the table. "Shall I call him now?"

Daniel shook his head. "We'll wait until the police get here."

*****

When the phone rang that morning, Kathryn answered without thinking.

"Kathryn Hazzard?" an unfamiliar voice asked.

"Yes." Too late, she realized that answering the phone was probably not the smartest idea.

"I'm just checking a story," the man's voice continued. "I have a report that your mother and father's marriage was rocky before her death—can you confirm there was violence in their marriage?"

Shocked, Kathryn sucked in a quick breath. "Of course not. My father...my father never... Who is this?"

He said the name of one of the more rabid tabloids, a paper that would print whatever the hell they wanted to, and wouldn't care about her denials.

"I don't have any further comment." She terminated the call. How could they think that? How could they attempt to blacken her father's name—wasn't it enough that Hazzard was being dragged through the mud? She rubbed her eyes, feeling the shake in her hands.

Before the phone could ring again, she took it off the hook.

At lunchtime, Kathryn made herself a sandwich, closed herself into the library, and switched on the TV. She selected one of the 24-hour news channels. A familiar sight met her eyes—the gates of Hazzard.

"Kathryn Hazzard returned to Hazzard Hall this morning," the newsreader said. "There is no comment from her or her representative yet." The newsreader shuffled papers. "Here's a recap on this story if you missed it earlier.

Model Amber Grey revealed last night she had been paid to attend a sex party at Hazzard Hall—one of England's private stately homes. Although Ms. Gray denies working as a prostitute, the fact that she was paid to attend this party is clear solicitation on Miss Hazzard's part."

Kathryn gasped.

The newsreader continued. "Next, Mike Britton met Miss Hazzard met on vacation in Greece. Mr. Britton sold his story of their passionate encounter to one of the British tabloids." The screen behind the newsreader changed from a picture of Amber Grey to a clip featuring Mike Britton.

"I just thought she was a regular girl, you know?" Mike said. "Neither of us wanted anything from each other but a quick lay—I don't regret a minute of our time together, she's hot as hell. I just wish she told me her real name."

Kathryn groaned.

"And regarding this developing House of Sin story, we have a guest someone who actually knows Miss Hazzard. Head of the local Women's Institute, Felicia May."

Kathryn's hands gripped together as she stared at the screen. *Felicia May.* Upstanding member of the community. A woman in her early seventies who had been a friend of her father's and a stalwart champion of Hazzard Hall. Everyone in the village respected Felicia, despite her snobbish attitude about *the right people.* In her eyes, the owners of the local big house should provide an example to the rest of the population, in all things. She held this outdated concept dearly. Kathryn's stomach churned as the camera zoomed out to see Felicia, dressed in tweed, sitting nervously on a chair next to the presenter.

"Thank you for joining us here this afternoon, Miss

May," the newsreader said. "Tell me, what are your thoughts about this scandal?"

Felicia May's thin lips pursed and her expression soured as though she'd been sucking on a lemon. "Well, I'm shocked, Amanda. I have known Kathryn Hazzard for her entire life. I was friends with her father, you know. When your researcher telephoned me this morning, I felt sure that there had been some mistake. I really couldn't countenance that these goings-on had happened at Hazzard Hall."

"We have received independent confirmation from another source," the newsreader said. "Unfortunately, it appears there can be no doubt that the house was used for a sex party. Although shocking, there is nothing illegal about this. What people choose to do in the privacy of their own homes is…"

"Her father would turn in his grave." Felicia grimaced.

"Indeed." The newsreader nodded, as if confirming Felicia's opinion verbally was not enough. "I think we are all shocked by recent developments. As I've said, there is nothing legal about holding a private sex party, but what *is* illegal is the procurement of women for sexual purposes. The police investigation is continuing, but if Miss Gray's accusations prove correct, Hazzard Hall has been used as a brothel."

Felicia's head shook from side to side as though every atom in her body was denying this scandalous possibility. "The sexual exploits of the latest Hazzard chatelaine shouldn't be allowed to destroy the strong and honorable legacy of previous generations. I really can't express my horror and upset at what Kathryn Howard has done." She looked as though she might cry.

"If you could say anything to Kathryn Hazzard, what would it be?"

Felicia breathed in deeply, straightened her spine, and stared straight into the camera.

Then she delivered the deathblow. "Shame. Shame on you."

Vires et vertutem. Strength and fortitude—the family motto carved into the wooden shield hung above the fireplace in the stone-blocked hall, and woven in the center of the family's fine, linen damask tablecloths—had never felt so out of reach.

Kathryn turned off the television; she pulled her knees up to her chest, curled into a ball, and started to cry. Everything she'd spent her entire life trying to avoid had come to pass. Seduced by the promise of easy money, she'd prostituted her home and destroyed her reputation. Worse, she tarnished her family name. Her home would forever be known as The House of Sin. Her reasons for taking the job were admirable, but that didn't matter now.

Daniel had made an offer that was difficult to refuse. When she'd wavered, he doubled it. Like the devil, he'd tempted her to sell her soul.

And she had. If she could turn back time—if she could foresee the consequences of the easy acceptance of his proposition—she would have known that no money was worth this.

I wish I'd never heard of Daniel Hunt.

*****

By early evening, sharing her house with a bunch of strangers was getting old. They were there for her protection, but she longed to be alone. All she wanted to do now was nuke a TV dinner from the freezer, pour a glass of wine and wallow in front of a mindless rom-com.

Something that was completely impossible to do when her house was full of men.

She walked out onto the front door step where he was having a cigarette break with another security guy. "Bill, can I have a word?"

He dropped the stub onto the gravel and ground it beneath his heel. She resisted the urge to tell him to pick it up and put it in his pocket.

He walked into the house.

"I appreciate all you've done," she said, "but I think I can handle it from here on in."

"I'm sorry, but I'm under orders not to leave you alone."

Daniel's orders. Even if he wasn't actually here with her, he was still controlling what happened in her house.

"I need to be alone." She crossed her arms. "Of course it would be madness to stay here without any security, but I need space." She reached into her pocket and pulled out the set of keys. "The Lodge at the gates is vacant at the moment. It has four bedrooms and is fully equipped. You will all be very comfortable there. I'll bring some food from the freezer to tide you over until tomorrow. The gates are locked. Once I'm alone I'll put on the burglar alarm." She pointed down the drive to the gate lodge, which looked like a small, Swiss chalet. "It's not far." She heard the pleading tone in her voice but didn't care. The past few days had been a trial that only being alone in her cocooning home could heal.

"Daniel won't like it."

"He doesn't have to like it—he just needs to tolerate it." She jiggled the keys.

Bill thought for a moment. Glanced over, with a calculating look on his face as if trying to evaluate the possibility of her changing her mind. She won. He took the keys from her hand. "Okay, we'll transfer things from the bedrooms and be out of your hair within the hour. We'll be back after breakfast tomorrow morning. Okay?"

She puffed out a relieved breath. "Great."

Chapter Twenty-Two

Daniel and Max had spoken to the police. An arrest warrant had been issued for Joel. And Daniel had spoken to Cain and Susan and apprised them of the situation.

Now, all he wanted was to be with Kathryn again.

Every time he called her cell, it rang out. So he sent a text. *Need to talk. Phone me.* When this went unanswered, he called Bill. "I need to speak to Kathryn," he said, not bothering with small talk. "Hand your phone over to her, would you?"

"She's not with me, boss." The security man's voice was apologetic. "She asked us to leave."

A mixture of fear and anxiety burnt through Daniel like acid. "What the hell do you mean? You work for me, remember? And I told you to protect her at all costs." His jaw was clenched so tight his teeth ached.

"Her security hasn't been compromised, but Miss Hazzard wanted to be alone in the house. She asked the security team to move into the gate lodge. From here, we can monitor the gate and the perimeter and be on hand in a moment's notice. She promised to put on the alarm the moment she was alone."

But she wasn't answering her cell…

Daniel made a snap decision. "I want you to go up to the house now and check she's okay. Once you're with her, phone me back and hand her your cellphone."

"Will do."

*****

Long, hot baths had always been Kathryn's own particular weakness. The shelf in the bathroom held an array of bath oils, bath bombs, and bath bubbles that would be the envy of any chemist's shop. All her friends knew of her penchant for bath products, and as a result every Christmas and birthday her collection was added to.

She squirted a generous measure of bath gel into the steaming water, and smiled in satisfaction at the floating, ever-growing foam of bubbles. Her cell phone had rung a few times—she'd seen Daniel's name and ignored it. The security team had no doubt contacted him the moment she threw them out, and he'd be calling to rant at her to reinstate them.

She didn't want to have that conversation. Didn't want to put her thoughts into words. They couldn't be together. She had to try and rebuild her reputation—the reputation of her house. And she still felt shaky and tearful at Felicia May's public condemnation on the news. When she talked to Daniel she had to be calm. Had to be resolute.

Had to end it.

She'd bathe, and then check in with Max.

She shed her towel and stepped into the bath. Lay back, so the water covered her ears, and closed her eyes.

An hour later, a half-drunk bottle of her father's favorite red wine sat on the coffee table. Kathryn cradled a glass in her hands, and stared at the TV. Even her favorite romantic comedy couldn't raise a smile, and the more she drank, the more morose she became.

She was desperate to talk to Max. But contacting Max meant she'd have to talk to Daniel. Today had been bloody awful. She'd been accused of running a whorehouse, her blameless father had been slandered, and her house was being referred to as *the house of sin*. Even Felicia May, a woman she'd respected her whole life, publicly condemned her.

She wanted him. Even now, the thought of escaping reality in his arms was damned tempting. She clamped her eyes tight shut, and remembered the last time they'd made love. *I made love,* she forced herself to accept. *He fucked.*

Last night she'd thought he might kiss her for a moment, but he'd told her to go to bed and walked away— he couldn't make his feelings for her any clearer than that. At least one of them had the brains to stop this madness.

Anger that she'd walked into this situation so stupidly replaced deadening despair. Anger she could direct directly at Daniel.

Her name, her house, her reputation. All ruined. For two million.

She'd sold out cheap.

She drained her glass and refilled it. *If I'm going to get legless, it might as well be on Château Margaux.*

The doorbell rang.

She ignored it.

It rang again. And again. Then whoever was there started hammering on the heavy mahogany.

Clutching her glass, Kathryn got up and stumbled to the door. She stared at Bill Waterstone through the bullet-proof glass. "What is it, Bill?" She held up her glass. "I don't want to see anyone this evening." She giggled. "I don't want to see anyone ever."

He frowned, and held up his cellphone. "Urgent call."

Another person wanting to torment me—I don't think so... She shook her head. "I'm not taking any more calls."

"Let me in, Kathryn." The look on Bill's face made it clear he wasn't going away, so she turned the key in the lock, unfastened the brass bolt and opened the door.

He thrust the phone toward her.

"This better not be another nuisance call," she warned him. "Hello?"

"Why the fuck are you not answering your cell?" Daniel's voice growled.

"Because I'm sick to death of being called a whore. Sick to death of people asking if my father used to hit my mother. Sick to death of everything." She swigged her wine. "Is Max okay?"

"Max is fine—"

"That's all I wanted to know." She staggered a little, and propped herself on the doorframe. "I don't have anything else to say to you, except leave me alone. I'm sick of you too."

She handed the cell to Bill. Waved him back from the front door, and locked it behind him.

*****

Max had organized a bodyguard to protect her against the threat of Joel, so with nothing else to do, Daniel returned to the hotel in the center of London. The 'house of sin' still dominated the airwaves, and after hearing yet another of Kathryn's quick lays on the radio, spilling details of their fling, Daniel had to act. He contacted Cain's publicity manager, and called for a press conference in the hotel lobby.

When the appointed hour came, he descended in the elevator. The moment the doors slid open, a throng of reporters clustered around him like pearls on elastic. Two cameramen pointed TV cameras his direction.

"Good morning. My name is Daniel Hunt and I have a statement. I will answer questions afterward so for the sake of clarity I would ask you to hold your questions until then." He stared into the unblinking eye of a camera. "There have been reports in the press and on television damning the owner of Hazzard Hall for her decision to rent the house to me for a private party. Her morals have been questioned, and her private life has been dissected cruelly and unnecessarily. I would like to put on record here and now that Miss Hazzard is not at fault. Under difficult circumstances, she has done everything she possibly could to save her house. Her integrity in trying to find a solution to the unbearable costs of maintaining house like Hazzard should be applauded."

He crossed his arms. "I persuaded her to rent her house to me for an evening. Everything that took place during that evening is my responsibility, not hers. Continuing to hound and berate her verbally or in print will result in legal action. Not instigated by Miss Hazzard, but by me."

A reporter who didn't look old enough to have left school, put up his hand, and when Daniel nodded, asked his question. "Did you employ prostitutes for your party? Solicitation is a crime."

Daniel scowled. "This was a private party, held on

private property by consenting adults. I'm sure any claims to the contrary will be fully investigated by both the police and the legal system. Once again, I wish to reiterate that Kathryn Hazzard is an innocent party in this matter."

The crowd was silent as he turned and walked away.

Now he'd given his name to the press, they'd turn up every dirty little secret he had and expose them to the light. The dysfunctional upbringing, the scandalous rumors at the time of their father's death, his whole, sordid childhood. They'd focus on Cain too. In defending Kathryn's honor, he'd left Cain open to gossip and scandal.

There wasn't a right time for them to be together. If their names were linked romantically, she'd never be able to regain her reputation—would never be able to continue with her life as it had been. Maybe she already realized that.

He waited for her to call him back.

Bill had reported that Kathryn had been drunk—and he couldn't blame her, the temptation to crawl into a bottle of booze was strong, and if his father hadn't been a drunk, Daniel might well have succumbed.

Instead, he waited.

One day.

Two.

Three.

On day four, he called her cell, but she didn't answer.

An hour later, Bill rang him. "The press has been gone for a few days, and Kathryn wants us to leave too."

Joel was still at large—the thought of leaving Kathryn alone…

"She's pretty insistent," Bill added. "She's busy. A team of workmen arrived this morning and a skip has been delivered outside the house. They are taking out all the additions that were made for the party. Her friend Max is here too, and has a bodyguard with her every second. A furniture van is due to arrive this afternoon to take out all the hired furniture."

She was getting on with her life. Without him. And there was damned all he could do about it. "Fine. Pack up the team and leave."

*****

The deal was done. For the past couple of weeks Daniel had concentrated on transforming an idea into a workable business. Sergei and Cain had both shown considerable interest in becoming investors in his jet charter business, and after meetings in both Paris and California a deal had been inked birthing Hunt Air.

Sergei's Learjet had been leased to Daniel's company, and Daniel had purchased another. He had three other pilots available on standby so whenever a client needed their services Hunt Air would be ready.

Running his own company was completely different from working for somebody else. He'd never felt so personally invested in his future—never wanted to work crazy hours. Both Sergei and Cain networked with other billionaires on a regular basis and already Hunt Air were receiving enquiries about the service.

He had decided on a very precise business model. One where a group of billionaires subscribed to Hunt air's services on a yearly basis. This cooperative would give its clients the best of both worlds.

They would have immediate access to state-of-the-art aircraft, flown by top class pilots and experienced in-flight staff whenever they needed it. The service would be tailor made to take into account each client's particular requirements and preferences, using Hunt Air would be just the same as owning their own planes.

But with one essential difference. There were no costs of ownership.

Should demand outstrip supply, the company could expand by purchasing more aircraft and employing more pilots.

Daniel worked hard, driving himself to exhaustion to escape the desire for Kathryn. Even when sleep claimed him he couldn't escape her memory. He dreamed of her face, of her body, of her taste. In his dreams, he breathed in her familiar scent, heard her husky voice. On waking, disappointment was the first emotion that buffeted him, followed with the painful ache of resignation.

The resolution to not contact her was damned difficult to keep. Just as anticipated, his press conference in the hotel had shifted the focus away from her and onto him. But still she remained silent.

He wanted to storm in there and demand she come away with him—but what was the point? Her precious house had always been her number one priority, he couldn't compete with a pile of bricks, and there was no way he would get down on his knees and beg.

No way.

After his last meeting in Paris with Sergei Daniel had retreated back to the house in Provence. He'd moved into the guestroom because, just as he'd feared, her presence was so strong in the bedroom they had shared there was no hope of a peaceful night there without her.

Chapter Twenty-Three

"Are you sure about this?" Max asked. "It's not too late to change your mind."

"I'm sure." In the previous three weeks, a team of painters and decorators had wrought wonders on Hazzard Hall. All traces of the party had been erased, and the worn bedrooms had been repainted and refreshed. She'd worked hard on evaluating all the furniture and furnishings too, keeping the essentials, and sorting the rest.

Some she would keep—and some would go to auction. The second million had been lodged in her account, but it was time for a new start, and she needed to declutter.

She'd thought long and hard about the future, and even though she had the financial means to stay in Hazzard she no longer had the desire to. There was a great wide world out there waiting for her, a different life to the one her father and generations of Hazzards had lived. She didn't want to be tied to the house any longer.

It had taken years to realize she didn't have to be.

"She's here." Max walked to the front door and opened it wide.

Felicia May's driver climbed out of the car, helped his employer from the back seat, and accompanied her to the front door.

She hadn't seen Felicia since the television appearance, but they had spoken on the telephone and Felicia had apologized for her condemnation of Kathryn's behavior. That initial contact thawed the ice, and Kathryn reached out to Felicia with her new idea for Hazzard's future. To her relief and delight, Felicia agreed to coming on board as a trustee, and fully supported the proposed new venture.

"Come on in." Kathryn took Felicia's arm. "Let's have tea, then I'll walk you through my plan."

Over the next couple of hours they wandered through the house discussing the changes that had been made and were still to make. Before Felicia left she turned to Kathryn at the front door. "Once again, I'm sorry I misjudged you. I know your father would be proud of what you are doing now."

Kathryn thanked her. She stood shoulder to shoulder with Max as Felicia climbed into her car and drove away.

"End of an era," Max murmured. She put her arm around Kathryn's shoulder and stared into her eyes. "I have to go check with my dominatrix and find out how our kidnap victim is getting on. Will you be okay alone?"

"I'll be fine." She never thought she'd see this day, never thought she'd be the one to leave Hazzard. There was a trace of sadness in her heart, but the overwhelming feeling was of relief and excitement. Now the question of the house was resolved, she was a free agent.

"You should call him, you know." Max was singing a familiar tune. She'd tried to engage Kathryn in talk about Daniel for weeks now.

"I want to." She'd ignored his calls, had stubbornly refused to talk to him, but the long, lonely nights had taught her a valuable lesson. Daniel Hunt was in her blood. The disaster that had befallen Hazzard hadn't been of his making—Max had confessed to sneaking Joel in, yet there was no condemnation of Max in Kathryn's heart.

And she had made the decision to hold the party on her own—he had offered an incentive that was darned difficult to refuse, but he hadn't pressured her. By reacting hastily she'd broken the ties with the man she craved. A simple phone call now wasn't going to cut it; she needed to meet him face-to-face.

"Cain says Daniel is miserable," Max said.

Max was in contact with Cain? "I didn't know you and Cain were talking."

"He's called a couple of times wanting to know how you are and complaining about his brother's bad mood. He told me he asked Daniel to come back and work for him but Daniel refused. He's gone into business for himself—a plane charter business."

"What did you tell him about me?"

Max grinned. "Only the truth—that you're miserable without him too."

"He could be anywhere by now…"

"I know exactly where he is. He moved back into his house in France. He was moaning that his brother is becoming a recluse. If you want to see him, go to France."

Will he accept me with open arms? Am I strong enough to survive if he turns away?

*****

Daniel drifted from deep sleep into consciousness. On opening his eyes his attention was immediately drawn to the thin sliver of light stretching from the open bedroom door. He always slept the door closed.

A figure stood in the doorway. Her face was in darkness but there was no mistaking her.

"Hi." His body came alive at the sound of her husky voice. For the first time in weeks, joy spread through him. She crossed the carpet to the bed.

They had a lot to talk about, but right now talking was the last thing on his mind.

He sat up—his back propped against the headboard. She wore a simple white dress, with buttons down the front and with each step she undid another one. Her gaze locked with his, compelling, magnetic, forming a link between them as strong as steel chain. His muscles tensed and he held his breath. The look in her eyes made his cock harden.

Jesus, I've missed her.

She shoved the dress from her shoulders and let it pool at her feet.

Daniel's heart hammered hard in his chest. In a white cotton bra and plain white panties she was more enticing than ever. Her face was naked of makeup and she wore no jewelry. She didn't need either.

She was close enough to touch. Daniel stroked a hand up her thigh, over her hip to her waist. His fingertips pressed into her flesh, urging her onto the bed. Their mouths met. He breathed in her scent, trailed the tip of his tongue over her lips then plundered them, closing his eyes and letting sensation pummel him like storm-force winds.

He'd thought he was doing okay without her, but having her in his arms brought home the realization that the past few weeks he'd been half dead.

He unfastened her bra and filled his hands with her.

She pulled down the sheet, revealing his nakedness, and curled her hand around his cock.

"I've missed you so much." She shimmied out of her panties and threw her leg over him, pressing her damp core against his hardness. "So much," she whispered, rotating her hips and grinding against him.

His thumbs flicked over her nipples. She moaned. He'd been so starved of the taste of her, for the sound of her. He should take this slow, should savor everything she had to offer. He wanted to put his tongue and his fingers inside her, but the way she was moving against him made that impossible.

He grasped her hips and moved her up a fraction letting his cock spring free.

"I've fucking missed you too." He positioned himself at her entrance and thrust into her. *This is what heaven feels like. The silken sheath of Kathryn's body.* She collapsed onto him and he wrapped his arms around her warm body, feeling her inner muscles tighten around his every thrust. She writhed, her breath coming in rapid little pants as their bodies found each other again, two halves of the same whole, separated too long.

"I love you." He felt her warm breath at his ear, her hot words in his head, and there was no holding back—no denying the truth as he shouted her name as he came.

What the... Daniel's eyes opened in the dark room.

He was breathing heavily, and the evidence of his wet dream was sticky on the sheets.

Christ almighty. He pushed a hand through his hair and groaned into the pillow. It didn't matter where he was, what room he slept in, Kathryn Hazzard had him by the balls. He sat up. Turned on the light. Climbed out of bed, and grabbed a towel on his way to the shower. He'd dreamed of her dressed in white cotton. Clean, unadorned and naked. Telling him she loved him.

He was totally messed up.

He turned on the shower, and stood under the streaming water. This couldn't continue. He was done with waiting for Kathryn—done with pretending he had a hope in hell of getting over her. The moment it was light, he was flying to England.

Their connection couldn't be faked, couldn't be escaped, even when they were apart.

She's mine. I'm hers.

And it was time to make sure she knew it.

Chapter Twenty-Four

The warm water soothed not just her body, but also her mind. This was still her home. Still her retreat from the world outside. Still special. Time was a healer, and already the scandal was fading into yesterday's news, helped greatly by Daniel's press conference a few weeks ago. She hadn't even thanked him for that—yet another thing to add to her *I'm sorry* list when she arrived in France. *Vires et vertutem.* Hazzards had endured through the generations. She would survive this.

Her nipples, poking through the bubbles, stiffened and chilled. A gust of air breezed through the room, but the windows and doors were closed…

Kathryn's eyes flickered open. Shock and fear struck through her. She shot up from the water, hands covering her breasts. A man stood next to the bath. A stranger holding a large knife she recognized from the knife block in the kitchen.

Unable to speak, she sucked in air.

He was dirty. Wild. His long blond hair was tangled and unkempt as if he'd been living rough. He wore a blue sweatshirt and a pair of battered jeans. The open bathroom door behind him was the source of the breeze.

"Where is she?"

She? Who... "How did you get in here?"

His mouth tightened. "I'm asking the questions. Where's Max?"

Joel. They'd never met, but this must be the man who'd strangled Susan. Kathryn had never felt more vulnerable in her life. Naked but for a film of bubbles, with no one in the house to protect her, and access to the telephone and the panic button on the alarm system out of reach.

He raised the knife.

"Max isn't here," she said. "I didn't need her to look after the house, I'm back now. Listen, just let me get out— let me get dry and changed and we can discuss this."

His gaze travelled over her shoulders and her breasts covered by her hands. "That would make you feel more in control, wouldn't it? You're frightened of me, aren't you, Kathryn?"

Terrified would be more like it. But she couldn't let him know that. "The water is getting cold, I'm uncomfortable. You have me at a disadvantage. I don't even know your name." She glanced behind him at the towel rack. "I need to get out. Please, pass me a towel." She waved toward the towel rack. "Are you hungry? Once I'm dressed, I can make you something."

He considered for a moment. "Fine." He snatched the thick, white towel from the rack and handed it over. "Make it quick." To her relief, he strode out into her bedroom.

*****

Daniel's Mercedes sped along the motorway. Despite Max's

supposition that Kathryn was in the bath or had gone to bed early, he couldn't shake the feeling that she was in trouble.

Traffic was heavy—it would take another twenty minutes before he reached Hazzard. He called Max again.

"Did you get through to her?" he asked.

"No, she's not answering her cell," Max said. "And the house phone is off hook, she hasn't done that since the media were hounding her." She sounded worried. "She's a light sleeper—and she always has her cell phone nearby. I'm beginning to think you might be right. She might be in trouble. I was with her today, but we're back in London now."

Daniel's curse turned the air blue. "How was she acting? Was she okay?"

Kathryn was level headed, he didn't really think she might have done something foolish, but she'd refused to take his calls, so he couldn't judge her state of mind. She'd been drinking when she threw Bill out of the house—maybe she'd…

"She was good," Max said. She hesitated for a split second. "She was talking about contacting you."

His hands clutched around the steering wheel. "She was?"

"Yes." He heard Max breathe in. "She…I know she cares about you."

Maybe she'd had that dream too.

"She always keeps the door locked and the alarm on." Max sounded as though she was trying to convince herself of Kathryn's safety. "The key for the front door is a hundred years old, and there is only one of them, there's no possibility of picking that lock, and she always shoots the brass bolt. No one could get through that. The windows at the back are locked and shuttered, and any that don't have shutters are covered with iron bars. The place is impregnable."

The glass panel in the front door. "There are no shutters on the glass in the front door," he mused aloud.

"Kathryn's father replaced the original glass with bullet-proof glass a few years ago as a security measure. There's no way of getting through it."

The turnoff to Kathryn's village was ahead. Daniel changed lanes and flicked on his turn signal. "Okay. I'll be there in ten minutes. If you don't hear from me in fifteen, call the cops."

*****

Joel was pacing the room when Kathryn came out of the bathroom. Luckily, she'd taken a large fluffy cotton terry bathrobe in with her, so she no longer had to face him naked.

The room was dimly lit from the small lamp on her bedside table. She'd always found subdued lighting relaxing, but not this time. "Shall we go downstairs? I could make you something to eat." Even though she was quaking inside her voice sounded calm and steady.

"No." He moved to the half-open window and peered through the net curtains. "Someone is out there. They've been ringing the bell, and prowling around. We stay here." Thoughts of who her potential rescuer might be rushed from her head as he took one of the two gilt bedroom chairs in the room, and placed it next to the bedside table. "Sit." He watched her as she did so. Then he pulled a jar of pills out of his pocket, shook a couple into his palm, and tossed them in his mouth.

Great. Paranoid, on the run, and self-medicating. A recipe for disaster.

"I know who you are—you're Joel, aren't you?" She needed to make a connection, to reassure him somehow.

He sat on the bed again. Ran one hand through his hair, holding the knife tight in his grip with the other. "I need to talk to Max. I bet that woman has been talking all sorts of crap about me." His teeth gritted and his eyes were wild. "I love Max. She can't believe these lies."

"Why don't I call her?" Her cell phone was on the bedside table. "You can tell Max your side of the story—make her understand."

If only she hadn't been so stupid. If only she just done as Daniel directed and left the security team in place.

"Where is the woman? The bitch trying to steal Max from me?"

How much does he know? "She…"

"Max left me a message saying she regained consciousness." A shrewd look passed over his face. "Don't bullshit me."

Ice froze the blood in Kathryn's veins. "Yes, she's awake. For a while there we didn't think she would wake up, but she did. She needs to convalesce."

Telling him the truth seemed to ease his tension a little. "She told you, didn't she? That I strangled her."

"I'm sure you didn't mean it—auto asphyxiation can be dangerous, it's so easy to get carried away, to apply too much force without meaning to."

"I meant to do it." His tone was flat. "I wasn't trying to give her pleasure, I was trying to kill the bitch. She took Max into that bedroom—she wanted my woman all to herself." His smile was twisted. "And now I've admitted it to you, you're going to have to meet with an accident."

"I'm Max's best friend. If you hurt me she'll never forgive you."

The doorbell rang again a couple of times, and the sound of someone hammering on the front door floated up from downstairs. "You can't escape from here. When I didn't answer whoever is outside will have called the police." Rising panic was evident in her voice.

The automatic outside light clicked on, bathing the sweep in light. Joel moved to the window again and peered out. "Shit. He's putting up a ladder." He tore both twisted rope tiebacks from the curtains. "Arms behind you. Now."

He grabbed her arms and yanked them behind her, knotting the rope around her wrists. The other rope he tossed on the bed. Then he flicked off the bedside lamp. In the darkness, he stepped behind her and pressed the long, cold, steel blade against her throat. "One sound and I'll cut you."

Her eyes readjusted to the darkness. Outside, the frigid light painted the trees opposite the house with splashes of white. Joel was so close with every breath she inhaled the sour smell of his sweat. The cold steel compressed her windpipe in a macabre rerun of what had happened in this house less than a week ago, one floor up. She had to warn whoever was on that ladder. Couldn't let them stumble into this situation unaware.

She opened her mouth to speak, but Joel jammed his hand over her mouth, and dragged the point of the knife against her skin. "Stupid," he whispered. "Fucking stupid. You're bleeding, bitch. Try that again, and you're dead."

She stared at the rectangle of dim light oozing in from outside. Her eyes widened. A head appeared. A familiar head. *Daniel.*

She shook her head from side to side, but Joel's hand pressed harder on her mouth, holding her still. Daniel shoved up the window, and climbed inside. He couldn't see her in the darkness—had no idea of the peril he was in.

Then Joel spoke, "Hi, hero."

Daniel's head whipped around. His eyes searched the room.

"I have a knife at your girlfriend's throat," Joel growled. "So you're going to do exactly as I tell you with no tricks. Close the window."

Daniel slipped the window closed. "You fucking hurt her, and you're dead. Turn on a light." His voice was laced with threat, as chilling as Joel's when he held his knife to her throat.

Joel reached over and turned on the bedside light.

"It's okay." Daniel was staring at Kathryn's face. His gaze flickered to her throat, to the beads of sticky wetness she could feel there. His jaw clenched tight, and he curled his hands into fists.

"Easy," Joel warned. "You don't want her cut again."

Daniel's head jerked in affirmation. "I guess you're Joel."

"You guessed right." Joel pointed at the ground. "Lie face down, hands behind your head.

Daniel did as he was told. "I don't understand why you're here. Hurting Kathryn achieves nothing. The police are looking for you. I called them when I couldn't get an answer from Kathryn. The sensible thing is to give yourself up. Hurting either of us will only make things worse for you."

Joel's laugh was wild—unhinged. "I have no

intention of surrendering. I came to see Max, to talk to her." The knife pressed against Kathryn's throat, and she gasped. "Please…"

"For Chrissakes, let her go. You're hurting her." Daniel's head was to the side, and his eyes blazed. "As you've doubtless discovered, Max isn't here. What do you want?"

"I want Max," Joel shouted. "I want you to call her and make her come out here. I need to talk to her."

"Fine," Daniel said. "If I call her, you let Kathryn go."

"No!" Kathryn exclaimed.

Joel snatched the other rope tieback from the bed where he'd left it, walked over and pressed his foot into Daniel's back. He grabbed Daniel's wrists and tied them behind his back. Then, he shoved the knife in his belt and walked to the bedside table. "This is convenient." He grinned at Kathryn as he balanced the heavy weight of the war club—brought back by Theodore Hazzard from his voyage to the South Seas in the 1830's—in his hands. "A perfect weapon. I guess you keep it by the bed just in case of emergencies?"

She did. Just as her father and grandfather had done before her. She'd always been comforted by the thought that the weapon was close at hand, but now seeing it in the hands of her enemy made her blood run cold.

"My cell phone is in my pocket," Daniel said.

Joel checked through Daniel's pockets until he located it, then found Max's number in the address book and called the number. Then he crouched on the floor and pressed the cell phone to Daniel's ear. "No bullshitting." Then Joel turned to Kathryn. "Don't try anything."

"Max? It's Daniel. I'm at Hazzard."

He listened to Max's response. "No, you can't talk to

Kathryn right now."

The sound of Max's voice bled through the phone. The words weren't audible, but her tone was loud and insistent.

"Yes, do that," he said in response to something Max said. "Right now, I need you to drive out here."

Joel grabbed the phone from Daniel's hand and pressed it to his ear. With a roar, Joel hit Daniel on the head. "Stupid asshole!" he yelled as Daniel toppled over.

Kathryn screamed. The force of the blow had rendered Daniel unconscious—maybe even killed him. Heart pounding, she strained against her bindings, struggling to get to her feet. The chair fell to the side, slamming her hip and shoulders against the floor.

Chapter Twenty-Five

"He tipped her off," Joel said in a flat, unemotional voice. He kicked Daniel's prone body, idly, as if kicking a can down the street. "The guy must think I have shit for brains."

He walked to the window and glanced out. "It's time for me to go."

Blood trickled from a cut above Daniel's eye. She couldn't tell if he was breathing. "Let me go to him..."

"No." Joel patted his pockets, and pulled out a lighter. "I need a distraction." He flicked the top, and a tiny yellow flame glowed at its tip. A slow, satisfied smile grew as he held the flame to the heavy brocade curtains. "Goodbye, Kathryn."

Fire. The most feared thing of all, to a house filled with wood, dried to kindling through hundreds of years. In horrified fascination, she watched the flames lick the golden fabric, racing up its length, devouring the cloth.

Joel slipped the lighter back into his pocket, walked out through the bedroom door and closed it behind him.

"Daniel," Kathryn shouted. "Wake up!"

He didn't move.

She tugged at the ropes binding her wrists, but they

didn't shift—freeing herself by force alone would be impossible. *Think*. The acrid smell of burning fabric filled her nose and throat. The black smoke made her eyes sting and water. Panic made her stomach sick, threatened to overwhelm her.

Across the room, closer to the flames, Daniel lay on his front. She had to remain calm, had to help him. She flicked her wrists forward and then back. There were no spindles on the chair—nothing to wrap the rope around—so he'd tied her wrists to each other, rather than to the chair. If she could lever up, she could slide her wrists up over the back of the chair…

Kathryn pushed her hips forward. Wriggled. Contorted her legs into an angle that would be impossible without her weekly Pilates class, and managed to place her feet on the edge of the chair seat. Her biceps ached; the inner skin of her upper arms felt bruised against the hard chair back. Gasping with the exertion, she pushed her heels back, gaining leverage.

The room was filling with black smoke now, curling and swirling over the white plasterwork on the ceiling. A flame leapt from the curtain to the draperies of the four-poster bed.

She gritted her teeth, and, with one forceful heave, pushed her feet down on the chair seat, and straightened her legs, tugging upward with her arms at the same time. *I'm free!*

Her legs shook, and her arms hurt, but at least she was off the chair. Breathing fast, she straightened the fingers on one hand, squeezing them together and turning the thumb into her palm to make her hand as narrow as possible. Then, with the other hand, she rolled the twisted rope down, forcing herself to breathe as the tight rope cut into her skin.

At the knuckles.

She wriggled and tugged, working the rope over the broadest part of her hand, and then cried out in relief as the rope slipped from her fingers.

She staggered to her feet. Crouching below the level of the smoke, she stumbled across the floor to Daniel. She pressed her fingers to his throat and found his pulse. "Daniel."

He didn't stir.

She needed to move him, and quick.

"Daniel." She rolled him onto his side and slapped his face. Still nothing.

The smoke was descending. She shoved her nose into the wrap collar of her bathrobe in an attempt to filter the worst of it out. Grabbed Daniel's ankles, and, sweat breaking out on her brow, pulled him toward the bathroom door.

It took a few minutes, but eventually she was able to shut the door behind them.

She dunked a couple of large towels in the cold bathwater still in the tub, and shoved the sopping material in the gap at the bottom of the door. Now the rush to remove Daniel from the path of the fire was over, she breathed until her heartbeat slowed a fraction. From the other room, a noise became evident. A low rumble, building to a dull roar. The fire had finished with the fabric, and started to consume the wooden bed.

*****

Daniel floated up to consciousness, aware of something cool and damp passing over his forehead. His eyes flickered open, and the first thing he saw was Kathryn's face.

She was hunched over him, clutching a damp washcloth. "Thank God," she breathed. "Can you get up? We have to get out of here."

With a quick glance, he took in the rest of the room. "Where is he?" His head hurt like fuck; exploring it, he encountered a lump the size of an egg. She helped him sit.

"He's gone. He set fire to the bedroom." She was remarkably calm considering the circumstances. "I dragged you in here. The door is hot to the touch now."

"The moment you got free you should have climbed out of the window onto the ladder." With fire blazing in the room next door they were effectively trapped.

"The police are outside moving the ladder now. There was no way I was leaving you." She reached for his hand. "You were unconscious."

The expression on her pale face stunned him into silence. She gazed into his face as though he was the most important person to her in the world. As if nothing else mattered.

Daniel cupped the side of her face and kissed her hard. He knew how she felt. When Joel had flicked on the light to reveal Kathryn with the knife pressed against her throat his heart had almost stopped. Filled with a primitive fury, he'd wanted nothing more than to kill the guy but hadn't been able to react for fear of jeopardizing Kathryn's safety.

Now was time to get out of there.

They scrambled to their feet and ran to the window. The sound of a siren could be heard, growing louder by the minute.

"I opened it a crack," she said. "I didn't want to flood

the room with oxygen, in case it fed the flames next door."

He ratcheted the window fully open, and peered out. "Hey!"

"Here," came an answering shout. "The ladder is secure. Come on down."

"You first." He slung an arm around Kathryn's shoulders, pulled her close and kissed her briefly. The heavy white robe was knotted around her waist. It might impede her movement, but as the only alternative was sending her down the ladder naked it would have to do.

"Are you okay to climb down? He hit you hard; I don't want you blacking out again. Maybe you should go first."

He'd spent his entire life looking after people—being the protector. She could have left him lying on the floor in her bedroom and climbed to safety, but she hadn't done that. Their roles had been completely reversed. "I'm fine." He jerked his head toward the window. "Sling your leg out and feel for the ladder with your foot." He held her tightly as she did so, breathing in her familiar scent.

"Got it." Her forehead creased in concentration as she edged her other leg out of the window, feeling around until both feet were at the top of the ladder. He gripped her upper arms, unwilling, unable to let her go. Then he shouted past her. "Kathryn is on the ladder. Can you climb up and help her?"

"On the way."

"Hold on, honey."

In a moment a policeman would help her down. Getting out of there, climbing to safety should be his only concern, everything else should wait. But he couldn't let her go before he told her the truth. "Take your time.

Concentrate and be safe. Don't put a foot wrong. I need you undamaged. Because I fucking love you."

*****

With cold gravel under her bare feet, Kathryn stared upwards. Pandemonium was breaking out. The police had responded, and two fire trucks had arrived. A team of firemen aimed a huge jet of water at the facade as a fire truck ladder inched up to the bedroom window. Another team raced in through the front door.

"It seems to be confined to your bedroom so far," the policeman who'd helped her down the ladder said.

Her gaze shifted to the flames in the window, and then instantly shifted back to the top of the ladder. "Can anyone shine a light up there?" she shouted.

One of the firemen did as she asked.

Daniel was edging downwards. She held her breath, silently praying that he wouldn't miss a step. When he finally reached the ground she ran to him, wrapped her arms around him and shuddered in relief.

"Stand back," one of the firefighters ordered. Moments later a cascade of glass showered from the bedroom window as the firefighters directed the stream of water into the fire's heart.

Her house was on fire. Maybe they'd be able to contain the blaze or maybe it all would be consumed. It was every homeowner's nightmare. Her arms tightened around Daniel, she rested her head against his hard chest and breathed in his scent. But he was safe. He was alive. His beating heart meant more than stone and plaster.

She grabbed the arm of a firefighter walking past. "I have to get something out of there. A portrait from the drawing room." She stepped away from Daniel. "Can I go in?"

"Better not, love," he said.

"It's really important—it can't get damaged."

"Where is it?"

"In the room straight in front of you when you go in. Above the fireplace. Please."

"Okay, we'll bring it out." The firefighter called over a colleague, and they disappeared into the house.

Daniel stepped close. With one finger under her chin he tilted her face up to his. "Did you hear what I told you?"

"The I fucking love you part?" She grinned.

"Yeah," he growled.

"Damn right, I did." She snaked her hands around the back of his neck. "I fucking love you too."

Chapter Twenty-Six

While the police questioned Kathryn, Daniel called Max. "We're okay." He opened the door of his Mercedes and sank onto the driver seat. "Kathryn's safe. Joel had her and set fire to the house. The firefighters are working to put out the flames now."

"Oh my God. Her poor house... And just when we'd... Are you sure she's all right? Can I talk to her?"

"She's giving a statement to the police. Joel got away. Make sure your security is alerted—he will try to get to you."

"Alexander never leaves my side," she said.

"There's no way we can spend the night in the house so we'll move into the gate lodge for the time being."

"I should come out there."

"No." In a few hours it would be dawn, they were both exhausted and there was nothing Max could do. "Leave it till morning. Can you bring her some clothes?" He looked over to the forlorn figure dressed in a white bathrobe. "And shoes. She doesn't have anything."

"Okay. I'll see you at around ten."

Next, Daniel called Bill Waterstone. "Sorry to wake

you in the middle of the night, Bill."

"What's happened?" Bill sounded instantly alert.

"The worst possible scenario." He explained what happened. "We've had one hell of a night of it, but she is safe." He stared at the blackened windows of Kathryn's bedroom. "Joel is still at large. He set fire to the house with us in it, and no doubt he reckons we're dead by now. I need you to reinstate the team; I'm not taking any chances."

"It will take me an hour to get to you."

Someone found Kathryn a pair of rubber boots and a blanket and they stayed outside, staring at the house until the fire was out and the firefighters left. Luckily, the fire hadn't spread out of Kathryn's bedroom—but the damage was extensive. Doors had been shut on the ground floor rooms, and their sturdy construction—with no gaps below or above—had shielded the rooms from smoke damage, but the rest of the house was a different story.

Her bedroom was a total write-off. The entire bed had been destroyed, and the fire had caused more than superficial damage—they would have to wait for a report, but it was likely that the floor and internal structure of the room would need extensive repair.

The foam and water the firefighters had used had caused a hell of a mess too.

Dawn streaked the horizon pink and gold when Daniel finally led Kathryn into the silent gate lodge.

"I'm too exhausted to even shower," she said.

"I'll help you." He propped the portrait of her ancestor against the wall.

She discarded the blanket inside the front door and took off the rubber boots so he unfastened the belt at her waist and let the rope drop to the floor. Taking her hand, he led upstairs. "You need to warm up." He turned on the shower, adjusted the temperature and helped her to stand under the streaming water. With a sponge, he washed her body. She stood still and silent until he was finished, then stepped out.

He wrapped her in a large white towel. "Where will I find sheets?"

"In the chest in the bedroom."

He kissed her gently, then went to make up the bed.

She trailed in his wake, exhaustion evident in her slow movements. When the bed was made he pulled an old T-shirt and pair of boxers from the bag he'd brought in from the car and handed them to her. "They are way too big but they'll do for tonight. I spoke to Max. She's driving out tomorrow morning and will bring you some more clothes."

"Thank you." Her voice was no louder than a whisper. She drew the T-shirt over her head and pulled up the boxer shorts. "Thank you for being there when I needed you." She climbed into bed and nestled under the quilt.

Daniel stripped, climbed in and curled around her. Her hair smelled of smoke. He stroked it back from her face and kissed her cheekbone at the hairline. "Go to sleep, honey." She didn't respond—sleep had claimed her.

*****

When Kathryn woke the following morning, for a moment, she didn't know where she was. She stared at the ceiling. *Am I dreaming?* She blinked, and her gaze shifted to the light streaming through an unfamiliar window.

She breathed in the faint trace of smoke and memory flooded back in a rush. *The fire. Daniel.* She turned in bed, but the space next to her was cold. Quickly, she got up and padded down the stairs.

She stopped at the bottom on seeing the portrait. "A different view for you, Tobias." He'd stared at the same four walls for decades—but everything changed. Everything was possible.

Daniel and Max sat at the kitchen table.

"Hey, you." Max was next to her in an instant, throwing her arms around Kathryn and hugging her tight. "We didn't want to wake you. How are you doing?"

"Exhausted." Being held in Max's arms was so comforting, she didn't want to let go. "The house…"

"I've been up there this morning, and I have a fire assessor arriving this afternoon," Daniel said. "The damage doesn't seem to be too bad."

"Come have some coffee." Max led her to the table, and then made her a cup and placed it down before her. "Thank God you're not hurt."

Kathryn cupped her hands around the mug. "If Daniel hadn't been here, I might well have been. I haven't even asked why you're here—"

Max looked from one to the other, then stood up. "I'm going to have a word with Bill." She walked out, giving them some privacy.

"I'm here because I can't stay away." Daniel leaned close, and grasped her hands. "I've tried being without you, and I can't do it. I know we want very different things in life—that you have a duty and responsibility to this house that you can't abandon, but somehow you and I have to make this work. I can't be without you any longer."

She stood, rounded the table and sat on his lap. She threaded her fingers through his hair and brought her face close to his. The truth of his words was in his eyes. She pressed her body against and spoke against his lips. "I feel the same way."

She felt him hardening against her bottom as they kissed. When his fingers slipped beneath the leg of the overlarge boxer shorts she groaned. "Come upstairs with me."

He quirked a dark eyebrow and deep dimples creased his cheeks. "Miss Hazzard, have you forgotten that your friend and our security team are just outside?"

"I haven't forgotten." She stood up and grasped his hand. "I just don't care."

The words she'd planned to say were unspoken. When they reached the bedroom, she closed the door and stripped off her clothes. "I've missed you." She walked into his arms, and ran her hands up under his shirt. Her fingers traced the bumps of his spine. Her head was against his chest, and she thought she could hear his heart beating. Perhaps it was just her heartbeat sounding in her ears. "I've missed you so much." She opened his shirt and pressed her mouth to his chest.

They tumbled into bed.

"I've dreamed of you," he confessed, cupping her breasts. "You've been haunting me."

He slipped a hand between her legs.

"I'm here now." She smoothed a hand over his hard hipbone, traced the dip formed in the honed muscles of his flank. "I don't want to be without you ever again."

Blocking out the world, they made love as lovers reunited after too long apart. Every touch, every taste, every sound, a reverent celebration of finding each other again. Nothing in the world mattered except having him inside her again, home where he belonged.

*****

After, she lay with her head on his chest with her arm curved around him. "I booked a flight to France—I was due to leave this afternoon," she said.

He angled back in an attempt to see her face. "What?"

She tilted her head back so she was looking into his face. Her mouth curved in a smile. "I'd decided I couldn't live without you too."

He kissed her. "What about the house?"

"I have...I had, a plan." Her fingers played with the light dusting of hair on his chest. "I decided I didn't want the responsibility of being the owner of Hazzard Hall to tie me to the ground any longer. I want to soar free. Over the past few weeks, I've set up a foundation with Hazzard at its core—my father got such comfort from being here while he was ill, I want to offer that same comfort for others who are suffering."

He stroked her shoulder.

"I've had help. One of my father's oldest friends, Felicia May, has come aboard as trustee, as well as my father's lawyer and another couple of people I trust. The house will be a retreat for people battling life-threatening illnesses. Not a hospice—we don't have the facilities to care for the terminally ill—but for those who need a couple of months to help them convalesce. Hazzard is such a special place—it has the power to heal. We have some sponsors already to help with the day to day costs, and I've invested some of the money from the party to start it off."

He winced. "The fire..."

"The fire is just a speed bump," she said. "We've been paying outrageous amounts of insurance for decades, I'm sure they will cover the repairs. Although I wish to hell I hadn't just redecorated upstairs."

She's free. She was on her way to France, to me.

Daniel hugged her close. "We'll fix Hazzard together." There was no way he was letting her out of his sight again. "Then I'm taking you away on holiday, and this time you don't get to say no."

Chapter Twenty-Seven

Kathryn guessed that as Daniel was so used to flying, being in the air for hours barely affected him. She felt wrung out by the two plane journeys, grubby and tired. Brazil was nothing like she expected. Her heart was in her mouth as they flew toward the tiny airstrip at Paraty, she was entranced by the thick rainforest, the curving strips of white sandy beaches at the rainforest's edge cutting into the sea, but terrified in equal measure. She'd clenched her hands so tight on landing that her nails had made tiny indentations in her palms. Daniel's smile was wide as he curled his hand over hers. They landed into a different world.

The buildings were painted powdery-white, the sound of birds was everywhere, and the air smelled fresh and clean, overlaid with the scent of the forest.

He hailed a cab to take them to the beach. She wished she wasn't so exhausted, because she longed to check out the beauty of Paraty firsthand. They drove past the ends of streets closed off with old chain stretching through ancient stone bollards. People walked the cobbled streets, or rode bicycles. The white painted terraces were enlivened by brightly painted doors, window and door casings painted too, in vivid shades of turquoise, red and yellows. It was early evening, and people dressed casually in jeans and shorts thronged the streets.

Daniel explained that the cobbled streets were too delicate for traffic, and in any case they had somewhere else to be, so she reluctantly accepted that they would have to leave exploration to another day.

They arrived at the glistening sea. Kathryn opened the door and sniffed the fresh sea air. Daniel paid the cab driver. "Not long now," he murmured as they walked to a row of brightly colored boats. She rubbed her hands over her upper arms, stared out over the water, and breathed in the salty scent of the ocean.

It had been a week before they managed to escape Hazzard, an eventful week. Joel had been captured on a train to London. A team of specialist architects had examined Hazzard and declared it structurally sound; the painters and decorators had moved back in.

The insurance company had coughed up for the repairs, and also had provided a lump sum to replace her wardrobe—going crazy with a credit card in a boutique had been fun with Max at her side.

"George is ready to take us to the house." Daniel grasped her hand and walked her to a man standing on the makeshift pier.

The two men talked as the brightly colored shallow-hulled boat sped over the ocean, following the coastline. They obviously knew each other well—their conversation was spirited, both of them laughing as they caught up. Daniel cracked a few beers from a cooler on deck and handed them out.

Kathryn sat on the worn wooden bench along the

side of the boat and trailed her fingers in the water.

After a while, Daniel joined her. He caressed the back of her neck, his long fingers digging deep into the muscles. She shifted so he could reach her more easily, and groaned as his large hands caressed her shoulders in long, firm strokes.

"Lean back." He linked an arm around her shoulders, pulling her against his hard chest. His breath was against her hair, his other hand still massaging her neck. She breathed him in, felt his body's warmth seep into hers and closed her eyes.

Now she wasn't looking at anything, her other senses became more acute. The only sounds were the steady thrum of the outboard engine and the slapping of water against the boat's sides. The air smelled sharp and salty, overlaid with Daniel's familiar scent. The touch of his hand stroking her upper arm, the warmth of his big body curled around hers, was so intimate it stole her breath.

"There!"

Kathryn's eyes flickered open to see George pointing at a gap in the thickly forested shoreline. A golden light bled from an isolated house in the darkness, fronted by a white beach.

"Casa Milagre," Daniel's deep voice vibrated through her. "We're here."

*****

Crested waves kissed the white sand, painted lace patterns of sea foam in ever repeating, dissolving arcs with the rise and fall of the waves. They said their goodbyes to George, and walked between blazing torches set in the sand to the house.

Daniel pushed open the full-length glass doors into

the open plan sitting room.

"This is incredible," she breathed. The wooden house was a modern build, faced totally in glass to take advantage of the spectacular view of the beach and the azure ocean. All the interior walls were made of glass. Above, an open walkway with a guardrail lattice made from rough-hewn logs stretched from the staircase to the bedrooms. The floor was tiled with large terracotta tiles, and dotted with Brazilian cowhide rugs. Heavy wooden bookcases filled with books lined an entire wall—Sergei was a voracious reader. A group of white covered sofas and low coffee tables made an attractive seating group on one side, and a carved wooden dining table and chairs graced the other. There were flowers from the forest everywhere, exotic blooms in vivid shades of a psychedelic rainbow.

A basket of tropical fruit was on the dining-room table, together with a silver ice bucket filled with melting ice and a large bottle of champagne.

"Something to drink?" Daniel opened it, pouring two streams of shimmering liquid into shallow champagne glasses.

"Mmm...." Kathryn joined him, sipping at the ice-cold liquid. "Who did this?"

"George called the caretakers just before we sailed." He trailed a hand over her soft cheek. "There should be food in the fridge, if you're hungry?"

She shook her head. "I'm beyond hunger. I just want to wash and get out of these clothes." She took another sip of the champagne. "God, this tastes good."

Daniel grabbed the bottle by the neck and handed it to her along with his glass, then picked up their bags. "Come, I'll show you upstairs."

She walked ahead of him, her hips swaying naturally with every step. He couldn't look away, as deep under her spell as a sailor bewitched by a siren of the sea. She was tired, needed to sleep after their long journey, but all he could think of was stripping her body bare and sinking into every delicious inch.

"The master bedroom is to your left."

She glanced over her shoulder and gifted him a smile that made his heart clench. What was it about this woman? His obsession with her was absolute, no matter how many times they made love he still wanted her more than he'd ever wanted a woman before.

She paused in the doorway, then stepped slowly in. "Wow." She stood at the foot of the impressive four-poster, swathed in white muslin that fluttered gently in the breeze from the open window.

When he'd stayed here after the death of his mother, he'd avoided this room, preferring instead to sleep in the smaller guest room. The beds were the same size, but this one was built for lovers; sleeping here would have only emphasized his aloneness.

He stacked their bags on the small luggage stand at the end of the bed.

"The bathroom is through there." He gestured at the door leading into the expansive bathroom, filled with a giant claw-footed tub, and state of the art shower built for two or more. "Will I draw you a bath?"

She handed him his glass. Refilled it, and hers too. Then placed the bottle on a nearby table. "If I have a bath now, I'll fall asleep in it," she confessed with a smile.

He slugged back a deep mouthful of champagne. "A shower then." Jesus, all he wanted was to peel off her clothing and take her to bed. He gritted his teeth and took a step away.

She ran her tongue over her lips. Pinned him with her gaze. "Where are you going?" Her voice was deeply seductive.

"I should leave you alone. Give you time to recover."

A dimple creased her cheek. "You could do that." She stepped closer, took the glass from his unresisting fingers. Drained hers, and placed them both next to the bottle on the table. "Or you could come to bed with me."

*****

She loved seeing the restraint leave his eyes. Loved the way he came to her, without a word, and cupped her face in his big hands and brought his mouth to hers. The snatched moments of intimacy they'd shared on the journey had been too brief—too tame. She wanted him, couldn't even think of sleeping or bathing when the prospect of having Daniel burned through her, setting her senses alight.

His tongue traced the seam of her lips, then slipped inside, rubbing against the top of her mouth then thrusting urgently, weaving a spell so erotic she shivered. She speared her hands through his hair, feeling his scalp under her fingers, barely aware as he unbuttoned her shirt.

Fumbling, desperate, he helped her shed the shirt and her light linen pants. Then he reached for her again, cupping her bottom in his large hands and pulling her up hard against his erection.

"Daniel." Heat pooled between her legs. *Oh, what he does to me, with only a kiss.* She shoved up his T-shirt as urgency took over. Urgency to have his naked skin under her fingertips.

With a wicked smile that revealed his killer dimples,

he eased away and tossed the inconvenient fabric across the room. Their gazes locked.

"I have something for you."

She'd thought he would pick her up, toss her on the bed, and fuck her until she couldn't see straight. To her surprise and disappointment, he walked away and picked up the small, silver flight case he'd carried from the plane.

"What's that?"

He sat on the bed and patted the space next to him. She sat.

"While you were shopping with Max, I had a meeting with a potential Hunt Air client, Lucien Knight."

The owner of the Gateway Club…

"I told Lucien of our escape to paradise, and he asked his assistant to give me this." He opened the case. "It's the connoisseur's collection of his company's products."

"Rabbits?"

"Rabbits, rings, and things you and I have never ever heard of." Daniel grinned. "State of the art fun. I could hardly refuse."

Daniel's eyes darkened. The smile disappeared. He undid his pants and stripped off the rest of his clothing.

His erection curved up to her, wide and hard. She traced the tip, feeling a bead of pre-cum on her fingers. She curled her hand around him and slid her hand up and down his length.

"Jesus, honey, that feels amazing."

Her nipples were so tight and aroused a shard of pleasure stabbed through her as he rolled them between his fingers.

Talking was too difficult, so she moaned instead.

"Get on the bed, honey." He took a long, silk scarf

from the case and joined her. "Arms up."

She looked behind her to the wooden bedstead. There was a carved panel above, and plain wooden spindles beneath. Daniel threaded the scarf through them, then took her hand and knotted the silken fabric around one wrist.

"I want to feel you," she grumbled as he did the same to her other wrist.

"You can do that later. Right now, I don't want you trying to stop me."

A thrill shot through her veins at what was to come. She tilted her head to the side, and raised an eyebrow.

"I'm going to eat you until you beg me for mercy. But I won't, because just when you think it can't get any better, that you can't come any harder, you will." He stroked his fingers down her stomach, into the cleft between her thighs. Rubbed over her stiffened clit, and dipping into the wetness beneath. "Jesus, you're so wet." He took her breast into his mouth, and sucked so hard his cheeks hollowed.

She wanted to hold his head to her, wanted to trace her hands over the hard muscles of his shoulders and rippling upper arms and wrap her arms around him, but unable to do so, she instead opened her legs as wide as she could and tilted her pelvis to press her dampened core against his cock.

His fingers slipped out of her, grasping his cock and rubbing it up and down—dipping into her then out, and against her clit.

"Fuck me," she groaned.

He shook his head and continued to lavish attention on first one breast then another.

Kathryn closed her eyes, feeling the rough brush of his beard at the side of her breast, then against her stomach as he kissed over the indentation of her belly button. His mouth was so delicious, so masterful. He knew exactly where to touch, was so attuned to her body he knew the brush of his mouth in the dip of her inner thigh drove her crazy.

So he did it again, this time licking her inches from where she wanted his mouth most.

Her arms tugged against the silken restraints.

He looked up, and the sight of his head between her thighs flooded her with moisture.. He pressed a kiss to the center of her, then reached for a pillow. "Up," he commanded, sliding the pillow beneath her bottom. "That's better." Both hands stroked firmly from her clit down her outspread thighs as he stared at her sex. "Are you ready, honey?" he whispered.

She sucked her bottom lip in. "I'm ready."

She could feel her heartbeat in her bound wrists, could barely breathe as his dark head lowered and his hot, wet mouth slanted over her core.

Kathryn closed her eyes and let sensation sweep her away. She didn't need the toys in the silver flight case—didn't need artificial aids to make her come, the feel of Daniel's mouth against her, the knowledge that she held his heart in her hands, was enough. Every day, every night, from here on in, he would be with her.

The bindings tying her to the past had been cut. The love she felt, she *shared* with Daniel had forged new ties. He owned her, body, soul and heart.

Familiar heat built as he wove his own particular brand of magic. She wanted to touch him, longed to. "Untie me," she moaned.

He looked up, his gaze burning with heat. "Come

first."

He rubbed his thumb over her, staring into her eyes as she lost herself, mesmerized as her chest heaved, her muscles quivered, and smiling the smile that twisted her heart as she totally lost control.

*****

Afterwards, they pulled back the sheets and climbed into bed. She was tired, and he could wait. Her head was on his shoulder, and he breathed in the scent of her hair.

"I want to redecorate the house in France when we get back."

"Really?" She looked up at him. "What did you have in mind?"

"I thought it could do with a woman's touch. The first thing I thought we could do is replace the tapestry over the fireplace with a kickass portrait."

Her eyes shone.

"Tobias?"

"Do you think he'd like to live there, with me?" It wasn't the question he'd wanted to ask, but she knew what he was asking, he could tell from her expression.

"I think he might." Her mouth curved into a sensuous smile. "What else is in that case?"

"There's a little bottle of magic liquid that apparently helps to prolong female multiple orgasms."

"I think I'd die if I added any more orgasms into my repertoire. With you, I'm insatiable."

The thought of the best way, the right way, the most unexpected way to ask her the question that burned within had tormented him for days now. He'd toyed with so many ideas but had discarded them all as cliché.

"There are toys for you in the case too, though, right?

You said something about a cock ring?"

"There are a couple of rings in the case. He leaned over the side of the bed, and dipped his hand into the case on the floor. "There's this one…" He picked up a circle of silicone with two thin strands arching from it. "I wear it, and it vibrates here," he touched the front of the ring, "against you. And this bit curves up between your ass cheeks and vibrates too."

Her eyes widened. She took the cock ring from him, and activated the hidden little button that set the ring to vibrate. "I like it."

"There's another one." He never thought this would be how he'd ask her, but hints about the portrait wouldn't cut it, and the time was right. He reached into the case where he'd stowed the little black velvet bag, picked it up, and handed it over.

"Interesting packaging," she mused, unfastening the black ribbon.

"To be honest, this didn't come in the case originally. It's from me."

She turned the bag upside down, and the emerald-cut diamond ring fell into her palm.

She gasped.

Fear briefly clutched Daniel's heart. They hadn't spoken of marriage, had only just admitted they loved each other. *Was it too soon? Might she say…* He breathed in deep. "I can't imagine being without you. I want you forever. Do you want that too?"

"Are you asking me to marry you?" She stared up at him.

"You have to ask?" He kissed the only part of her face he could reach without moving—the curve of her brow.

"Yes, Kathryn. I am asking you to marry me, and stay with me forever."

She slipped the ring onto her finger, scooted up so her mouth was close to his. "Home isn't a big house in the country, home is with you."

THE END

Thank you for reading Hazzard Blue!
I'm working on my next book, which will be out later in 2015.
x Tabitha.

Acknowledgements

I'd like to thank my family, for putting up with me while I wrote Hazzard Blue. I'd also like to thank my friends who waved pom-poms as I wrote, most especially the wonderful Zara Cox, and the fabulous Kitty French.

Without you both, I would still be thinking about writing an erotic romance, not the proud writer of one! Extra thanks to Kitty for not only allowing me to use The Gateway Club in the story, but also for helping me so much with promotion.

Printed in Great Britain
by Amazon.co.uk, Ltd.,
Marston Gate.